DEATH ON THE STELLA MAE

A KIPPER COTTAGE MYSTERY

JAN DURHAM

INKUBATOR
BOOKS

Published by Inkubator Books
www.inkubatorbooks.com

ISBN (eBook): 978-1-83756-109-4
ISBN (Paperback): 978-1-83756-110-0
ISBN (Hardback): 978-1-83756-111-7

Jan Durham has asserted her right to be identified as the author of this work.

DEATH ON THE STELLA MAE is a work of fiction. People, places, events, and situations are the product of the author's imagination. Any resemblance to actual persons, living or dead is entirely coincidental.

1

The first crash of thunder was so loud it woke Liz McLuckie. She opened her eyes, heart thudding, wondering what had disturbed her. The mystery was solved moments later when lightning ripped across the roof window, etching the beamed ceiling of the attic room with light.

'What...?' murmured Benedict Ossett. 'What was that?' He rubbed his eyes.

'Lightning. A storm.'

'Oh.' Unimpressed, he rolled over and went back to sleep. Liz supposed that in his decades in the navy he had seen hundreds of storms, many of them life-threatening. He knew he was in no danger tucked up in Liz's cosy bed.

She waited for the next crash of thunder. Even though she knew it was coming, it still made her flinch. The lightning followed straight after, magnesium bright. The sky hung black and bruised outside the window, taking a breathless pause, gathering strength. After a couple of minutes, the rain came. It started slowly – a few sploshes on the glass – and then grew steadier, increasing until there was a steady percussion. The wind picked up, seemingly from nowhere, making the window rattle and the chimney moan.

Liz snuggled back under the duvet, finding the shelter of Benedict's arms.

It took a bit of getting used to, being in a couple again after so many years alone. Her husband, Mark, had died five years before. Being forty-six at the time, she had genuinely thought the romantic part of her life was behind her, but what had started as a friendship with Benedict the year before had ripened into something more. The sexual attraction between them was an unexpected and thrilling bonus.

The rain continued to lash the window, accompanied by the occasional patter of shale from the cliff above. Thunder rumbled overhead, and a gust of wind sent something crashing to the ground outside. A roof tile, probably. Liz had bought Kipper Cottage and its neighbour, Gull Cottage, eighteen months before. She'd done them both up, and was now living in Kipper and renting out Gull, the larger cottage, as a holiday let. The storm was putting her renovations to the test.

A horrible thought occurred to her. She sat up.

'What?' said Benedict, without opening his eyes.

'Benbow,' she said. 'Do you think we secured that tarpaulin properly?'

'I'm sure we did.'

Liz lay down. Then sat up again. 'What if we didn't?'

Liz's friend Iris had accidentally flooded her cottage, Benbow Cottage, a couple of months before, and it had brought down her bedroom ceiling. When Iris moved into a retirement home, her son, Irwin, had decided to do some renovations to the cottage at the same time as the repairs. Liz had agreed to project-manage the work.

'What if the tarpaulin's come loose?' said Liz. 'The rain will be getting in. That ceiling might come down again.'

Benedict gave in and sat up beside her. 'I'm pretty sure we

tied it properly. But I can go and check if it'll make you feel better?'

'I'll come with you.' The idea of going out into the storm wasn't particularly appealing, but she knew she wasn't going to get back to sleep until she'd made sure everything was okay. She couldn't let Benedict go on his own: it was her responsibility.

They both dressed and made their way down the narrow wooden stairs to the ground floor. As they passed the bedroom on the second floor, Liz listened for any sound of Niall, her young friend and lodger. She heard nothing. She needn't have worried that the storm had disturbed him – his facility for sleep was legendary.

When they got to the kitchen, Nelson, Liz's English bull terrier, opened one piratically patched eye and peered at them from his basket. He watched them put on their water-proofs, then sighed and closed his eye again, resigned to the folly of humans.

Outside, the violence of the storm took Liz's breath away. Rain whipped her face, and a gust of wind blew her hood down, threatening to tug her off her feet. Benedict put an arm around her.

'Keep to the side of the street!' He had to shout to be heard over the wind. 'We don't want to be struck by lightning.'

Benbow Cottage, their destination, was in Neptune Yard, at the foot of the 199 stone steps that led up to the medieval abbey on the clifftop above the little fishing town of Whitby. It was usually only a minute's walk from Kipper Cottage, but it took much longer than that to get there as they struggled to stay upright in the wind and rain. When they reached the iron gate that led through a tunnel to the yard, they found it swinging wildly on its hinges. They latched it properly as they went through. There was a brief respite in the tunnel, and then they were buffeted once more by wind and water.

There were half a dozen cottages in the yard, arranged in a higgledy-piggledy fashion, some side-on and some facing each other across the square. Iris's cottage – Benbow Cottage – was the first on the left. When Liz saw it, she gasped in dismay. Three corners of the tarpaulin on the roof, secured by Benedict's sturdy sailor's knots, were still in place, but the fourth – the one she was supposed to have tied – had come loose. The tarpaulin was billowing with each gust of wind, rippling over the roof tiles, the rope whipping around dangerously. She knew they had to fasten it again quickly before the rain or the rogue rope could do any damage.

Liz fumbled the key in the lock with numb fingers. They hurried to the top floor, where Liz opened the window and leaned out. The end of the rope was flailing wildly. Liz made a couple of unsuccessful attempts to grab it. Lightning flashed.

'Let me try,' shouted Benedict, over the wind. He squeezed past her.

Liz had a horror of playing the helpless female, but in this case she knew she had no choice. Benedict had a longer reach, and – as she'd just discovered – his knots were far more reliable. He hung out of the window, lashed by rain, and finally managed to catch the rope. He secured it to the iron staple, tugging it hard, making sure it wouldn't come loose again, then ducked back into the cottage and closed the window.

'I think that should do it.'

Liz grinned.

'What?'

His dark hair, streaked at the temples with silver, was plastered across his skull. There was water in his eyelashes and running down his lean cheeks.

'You look like a drowned rat.' As soon as she said it, she realised she would look no better. She could feel water running off her hair, dripping down the neck of her cagoule.

He grinned back at her. 'Talk about the pot calling the kettle black.' He pulled her to him and kissed her. His lips were cold, but sent little shivers of pleasure through her. 'Come on, pot,' he said. 'Let's get back to bed.'

THE NEXT MORNING the storm had gone. Liz decided not to take Nelson up onto the clifftop for his usual morning walk, but took him instead to Tate Hill beach. The wild weather hadn't left too much of a mark on Henrietta Street – there were only a few smashed terracotta roof tiles on the cobbles, and a satellite dish swinging on its wire at number six – but down on the beach it was much more obvious. Although the sea was now as smooth as pewter, the high-tide mark lay thick with debris – smashed wood, seaweed, lengths of rope, a couple of crab pot buoys and even some dead fish. When Liz let Nelson off his lead, he ran straight over to investigate. As always, Liz marvelled at his ability to run at all. His head was so large compared to his body that Liz always half expected him to topple forward onto his nose. Some unkind people liked to call him the ugliest dog in Yorkshire, but Liz loved him.

She watched him affectionately for a few moments, then took a deep breath. Everything felt fresher after the storm, and there were definite hints of soil and vegetation in the salty air. Spring was coming.

She heard a sound across the water and looked to see where it was coming from. A fishing trawler was coming into the harbour, moving slowly around the pier, its engine sputtering. Liz felt sorry for the poor trawlermen having to be out in the storm. Trawling wasn't just a business, it was a way of life, hard and often dangerous. The trawler limped its way to the dock on the opposite side of the harbour. Liz was close enough to see the men on board hurrying to secure the ropes. She squinted. She could also see blue lights flashing on the quayside. There were a couple of police cars parked there, which looked as if they were waiting for the boat. But maybe not. She was willing to bet there had been quite a few disturbances in the town overnight.

'Come on, Nelson.' She coaxed him away from an interesting pile of seaweed and clipped him onto his lead. 'Let's go home.'

They headed off the beach at Tate Hill pier, up Tate Hill beside the Duke of York.

As they emerged at the bottom of the abbey steps, another figure appeared from Church Street.

'Morning, Mrs Mac. Morning, Nelson.' It was Mike Howson, dressed as usual in his high-vis vest. Uncharacteristically, however, he didn't have his fish trolley with him. He saw Liz's questioning look.

'No herring today. I'm just on my way to give the smokehouse the bad news.'

They headed up Henrietta Street together.

'The *Ocean Star* didn't go out at all yesterday,' he explained, 'and the *Stella Mae*'s still out.'

'I think I've just seen her come in.'

'Have you?' Mike looked relieved. 'She should have been in hours ago. Lesley's been worried sick about Billy.'

Billy was one of Mike's two sons. They were both involved in the fishing business, Billy on the trawlers, and the other, Sandy, in Mike's wet fish shop on Baxtergate.

Mike grinned. 'Now the lad's back, I can relax a bit.'

Liz wondered if she should mention the police cars, but decided not to. They might have had nothing to do with the trawler, and there was no point scaremongering.

'Things got a bit hairy last night, eh?' said Mike.

'Is there much damage in the town?'

'Mostly just broken windows and smashed tiles. A chimney stack came down on Salt Pan Well Steps. Old Grunty Gillespie's lost his fishing coble, but he probably didn't tie it to the pontoon properly. I daresay it'll turn up somewhere. Oh, and some of the lights have come adrift on PennyCity arcade. What about you? Did Kipper and Gull survive?'

'They're fine.' Liz was about to tell him about her adventures at Benbow Cottage, when she stopped. She could hear footsteps behind them, moving fast. They both turned. Mike's wife, Lesley, was hurrying after them, red-faced and puffing, her jacket pulled hastily over her fishmonger overalls.

Mike went pale when he saw her. 'Is everything alright?' he demanded. 'It's not Billy?'

Lesley shook her head and took a moment to catch her breath. 'No, not Billy... Doc. Catriona's Doc. He's gone overboard.'

2

Eternal Father, strong to save,
Whose arm hath bound the restless wave,
Who bid'st the mighty ocean deep
Its own appointed limits keep;
O hear us when we cry to Thee,
For those in peril on the sea.

L iz wasn't religious, but the words of the seafaring hymn, lifted to the ceiling of St Mary's church on the voices of the trawlermen of the *Stella Mae* and the *Ocean Star*, almost moved her to tears. The church was filled to bursting with people, squeezed into the eighteenth-century wooden booths, and standing three and four deep in the aisles. Liz had only just managed to find a seat at the back. She was on her own, because Benedict and Niall both had to work that morning, but she could see many people she knew in front of her. Mike and Lesley Howson, and Billy and Sandy were with Mike's best friend, Earl, and his daughter,

Catriona, Daniel Holliday's widow. They occupied the box
directly beneath the pulpit. In the box beside them sat
museum curator Dora Spackle, her usual green cloche hat
swapped for a black velvet one. Liz had been surprised to
hear that Dora was Daniel Holliday's aunt – she hadn't
realised that Dora had relatives in the town, because she
always seemed to be on her own. But perhaps that wasn't
surprising – she wasn't the easiest person to get on with. A
few rows back from the front, Liz could see her friend Tilly
and her wife, Mags, who owned the local café. Tilly had been
born in the town and had gone to school with Daniel. She'd
been curiously close-lipped about him in the three weeks
since he had fallen overboard from the *Stella Mae*, but had
told Liz she would be here.

The service was a memorial service, not a funeral, as
there was no body to bury. That wasn't an unusual state of
affairs in the little fishing community. Visitors to the town,
scrambling among the tombstones in the graveyard, would
probably be shocked to know that many of the graves were
empty – symbolic tokens of lives lost at sea.

Everyone sat when the hymn ended. The interior of the
church was a fascinating mix of original medieval gothic and
Regency fantasy, with barley twist columns, old-fashioned
booth pews, and an unusual three-tiered pulpit canopied in
velvet. The new minister, the Reverend Wishart, addressed
them from the middle tier. Liz thought how strange it was to
see him there rather than the Rev Gillian Garraway. Gillian
had left Whitby just after Christmas. She'd said it was
because she'd been made an offer she couldn't refuse by the
diocese, but Liz suspected it had had more to do with her
short-lived romance with Benedict. Liz had liked Gillian, but
she couldn't help but suffer a twinge of jealousy whenever
she'd seen her and Benedict together.

After finishing his first reading, Reverend Wishart called

on the captain of the *Stella Mae* to give a eulogy. Skipper Masterson was the epitome of a seafarer – a huge, bearded man with a stern gaze. He stood in the lower pulpit, uncomfortable in his suit and tie, reminding Liz of a wild sea creature tamed to perform. He didn't say much. Most of his remarks about Daniel Holliday – or Doc, as he was better known – were vague. He was a hard worker and could always be relied on when things got wild on deck. He loved watching boxed sets of TV shows, and gardening. It was curiously impersonal for a eulogy, but Liz guessed that the skipper was unused to speaking in public and to expressing his emotions. He was, after all, a Yorkshireman.

When the skipper had finished, there were several subdued cries of 'hear, hear!' from his crew. Most were faces Liz had seen in and around the harbour. One she knew well – the small but chunky Potsy Potter, maybe not the brightest spark in Whitby, but easily the most amiable. As the skipper rejoined the crew in their box, Potsy clapped him on the back.

Reverend Wishart cleared his throat. 'Thank you, Mr Masterson, for that moving tribute. Now let us sing hymn number 247 together – "Amazing Grace".'

The organ played the opening chords, and everyone stood. As she got to her feet, Liz's gaze landed on an unusual figure standing near the door. The woman was dressed all in black, which was hardly surprising, but also – anachronistically – in a veil that hid the whole of her face. Rather than making her anonymous, as the woman had probably intended, it had had the opposite effect – she was attracting curious glances from the other members of the congregation. Liz wondered who she was, and why she was dressed so dramatically.

Amazing grace, how sweet the sound

That saved a wretch like me

Liz wasn't a Christian. She was, however, a Scot. She could never sing or hear the words of that particular hymn without her imagination supplying a bagpipe accompaniment and a sentimental lump rising in her throat. When the hymn ended, they sat again. Liz glanced towards the woman in the veil, only to see that she had gone, having taken her chance to slip out the door. The Reverend Wishart cleared his throat again and looked down at his Bible.

'*I love the Lord, for he heard my voice—*'

The door burst open, framing a figure in the doorway. Liz recognised Grunty Gillespie, the old man who had lost his coble boat in the storm. He was wild-eyed and breathless with excitement.

'I've found him! He's on the beach!'

There was a beat of shock and then... uproar. Everyone spoke at once.

'What?'

'What does he mean?'

'Is it Doc?'

'Which beach?'

'Come with me!' yelled Grunty. 'I'll show you!' He bolted out again.

Catriona Holliday jumped up and ran out of her pew, followed closely by her father and all the Howsons. Dora Spackle sat for another shocked moment before leaping up and following them. Everyone streamed out of the church behind them, leaving the Reverend Wishart standing in the pulpit with his mouth open.

Liz waited in the graveyard for Tilly and Mags. They both looked grim as they came out of the church and joined her.

'I'm not sure it's a great idea for Catriona to go down there,' said Mags, crinkling her black brows. She was as dark as Tilly was fair – yin to Tilly's yang. 'He's been in the sea three weeks.'

'Hopefully her father will have the sense to keep her away,' said Liz.

'Hopefully.'

The congregation streamed down the abbey steps, following the general charge to Tate Hill beach. Usually, Liz liked to stop to take in the view of the town from the steps, but today she wasn't given the opportunity. She was swept along by the general press of the crowd.

'What did you think of the service?' she asked Tilly as they descended.

'Better than he deserved.'

Liz was taken aback. It wasn't like Tilly to be harsh or judgemental. Her stern expression didn't encourage further conversation, so Liz decided not to press her.

When they reached the bottom of the steps, they followed the crowd past the Duke of York and down the hill to the edge of Tate Hill beach, where everyone had stopped a respectful distance from the scene unfolding at the water's edge. Grunty Gillespie stood over something a hundred yards away on the stony beach, something yellow, tangled in seaweed. Liz knew that many of the fishermen wore yellow oilskins. The crowd fell silent, watching.

Earl joined Grunty, looked down, then quickly retreated to intercept Catriona before she could go any farther. He said something to her, and she hid her face in his chest. He put his arms around her, and Lesley Howson joined them. She put her hand on Catriona's shoulder. Mike Howson and his boys ventured farther, to join Grunty. They stood motionless, staring down at the heap of oilskin.

'Let us through, please. Make way!'

Several uniformed police officers shouldered their way through the crowd. They included Constable Bill Williams –

or Double Bill as he was known by his colleagues at the station – and were followed by a taller figure dressed in a puffer jacket and jeans. Detective Constable Kevin Ossett caught Liz's eye as he passed, and frowned.

Everyone watched silently as the policemen joined the little group on the beach.

'What the hell are you all doing here?' A sharp voice sliced through the crowd, and everyone parted to let Detective Inspector Fiona Flint through. She stood with her hands on her hips in her expensive skirt suit and trainers, glaring at everyone. 'Go home. This isn't a bloody circus.'

Everyone ignored her and turned back to watch the scene on the beach.

She rolled her eyes. 'You people.' Flint had come to Whitby the year before, from the tough streets of Middlesbrough. She hadn't exactly taken the town to her bosom, and the feeling was mutual. She stomped away over the beach to join her colleagues, Catriona and her father, and the Howsons at the water's edge. Liz saw that Dora Spackle was also there, standing a little apart from the others, her shoulders slumped, a handkerchief clutched in her hand. Even though Dora was difficult – prickly at best and downright obnoxious most of the time – Liz couldn't help but feel sorry for her. As far as Liz knew, Daniel Holliday was her only relative.

'Is it him, do you think?' asked someone behind Liz.

'Who else would it be?' answered someone else.

'I think it must be. Look, Catriona's crying. Poor thing.'

Sure enough, Catriona still had her face buried in her father's chest, and her shoulders were shaking. Flint was waving her arms at Bill Williams, clearly berating him about something. After a moment or two, he detached himself from the others and crunched his way back up the beach towards them. He flapped his hands.

'Go on, everyone. Go home.' His long face looked even more mournful than usual. 'Let us get him into the ambulance with dignity. You can read all about it in the *Bugle* tomorrow.'

LIZ RETREATED with Tilly and Mags to their café on Sandgate. The Full Moon Café had been a chip shop when the two women had bought it, and it had been in a terrible state. It looked very different now. It had a bookshop at one end and a spiral staircase that led up to a reading nook with battered leather chairs. The other end of the room had several tables and a big pine counter displaying home-made cakes. It was all decorated with an eclectic assortment of antiques – melamine tables mixed with wooden ones, lava lamps with old-fashioned fringed standing lamps, and a neon sign that said 'Stardust'.

Gryzna, their statuesque assistant manager, looked up from a copy of *Hello!* magazine as they came in. Her only customers were Iris Gladwell and her friend, ex-jockey Dickie Ledgard, who were eating scones.

'HOW WAS IT?' shouted Iris as she spotted them. When Liz had first met Iris, she'd thought the old lady was deaf, but it had turned out she wasn't – she was just incapable of speaking at any volume less than a bellow. Luckily, Dickie *was* deaf, in one ear, which might at least have partly explained why the two of them had hit it off so well.

'Is it over already?' he asked. 'That was fast.'

'DID THEY GIVE THE LAD A GOOD SEND-OFF?'

'In a manner of speaking,' muttered Mags. 'Until he came back again.'

'WHAT?' Iris's eyes opened wide.

'What are you talking about?' demanded Gryzna. 'How so, came back?'

As Mags told them about the dramatic turn of events, Liz gently steered Tilly to one side.

'Are you okay?'

Tilly pulled a face and ran a hand through her cropped blonde hair. 'What makes you think I'm not?'

'What you said about the service. About it being better than he deserved.'

Tilly sighed. 'I shouldn't have said that.'

Liz waited for her to say more, and eventually she did.

'Daniel Holliday was a bully.'

'At school?'

'I can't imagine he changed much.'

'He bullied you for being gay?'

'I didn't take it personally,' said Tilly. 'He bullied everyone.'

Liz frowned. 'I don't understand. Why were there so many people at his memorial?'

'It's a solidarity thing. A Whitby thing. Anyone who dies at sea, everyone goes, particularly the fishermen and their families.' Tilly shrugged. 'It could be any one of them next.'

They rejoined the group.

'I DON'T ENVY WHOEVER IT IS HAS TO IDENTIFY HIM,' said Iris.

'I imagine that could be done by the teeth,' said Gryzna. 'If necessary. But I pity his poor wife.' Gryzna was also a widow. She'd never told Liz exactly how her husband had died in Belarus, and Liz hadn't pressed her. Some things were better not to know. 'Does he have any children?'

'I don't think so,' said Liz. As far as she knew, Daniel and Catriona were childless.

'What?' asked Dickie. 'I didn't get that.'

'THEY DIDN'T HAVE KIDS,' summarised Iris.

'Aye, well,' said Dickie. 'Thank God for small mercies, eh?'

Gryzna nodded. Her twin boys were notorious in the

town, always getting into trouble. But all the same, Liz knew Gryzna wouldn't change them for the world. She'd put her own life on the line to get them into the UK when they were just babies, and, after handing herself in to the authorities the year before, was now waiting for the Home Office to assess her case. No one was too worried about it. As the boys had been in the country for more than ten years, they were automatically British citizens.

The bell on the door tinkled as it opened. It was Niall FitzGerald, Liz's young Irish friend and lodger, his hair sticking up in tufts as usual, blue eyes wide with curiosity.

'I've just got back. I hear there's been some excitement. What's happened? What did I miss?'

3

'You've missed a bit, just there.' Liz pointed to a patch just under the window. Niall hurried to touch it up with his brush.

'There,' he said. 'That looks grand now.'

They stood back to admire their work. The water damage to Iris's bathroom floor had been repaired, and the missing roof tiles replaced, which meant that Benedict had been able to take off the tarpaulin. Liz and Niall had given the ceiling and the walls a fresh coat of paint. It probably hadn't looked so good in a long time.

There was a knock on the bathroom door. 'Tea break?' It was Irwin, Iris's middle-aged son, dressed immaculately in a tweed suit and shirt and tie, covered by a floral apron. He was carrying a tea tray.

'Actually, I think we're just about done,' said Liz.

'All the more reason to reward you both.'

They all sat on the floor on the landing while Irwin poured them tea and gave them both a slice of freshly baked Victoria sponge cake. 'I can't tell you how much I appreciate this.'

'Don't be daft,' said Niall. 'That's what friends are for, isn't it, Liz?'

Liz nodded. She would have spoken, but already had her mouth full of cake.

'Busy day after this?' asked Irwin.

Liz swallowed her delicious mouthful. 'I have some new guests arriving at Gull today.'

Niall pulled a face. 'Hardly weather for a holiday.'

The squalls had continued ever since the storm. It had been just over a month now, and Liz couldn't remember the last time she'd seen the sun.

'I don't think they'll mind the weather too much,' said Liz. 'He's an RNLI man, out of Great Yarmouth.'

'A busman's holiday,' said Niall. 'You'd think he'd want a break from the sea. Feel some sunshine on his shoulders. I know I do.'

Irwin looked thoughtful. 'Something odd just happened. I was filling the kettle at the sink when I saw Dora Spackle come into the yard. She stopped at the door and knocked. I dried my hands and went to open it, but she'd gone.'

'Gone?' echoed Liz.

'Left again.'

'How odd.' It had been four days since Liz had seen Dora at the memorial service. Liz wondered how she was taking the discovery of Daniel's body.

'Odd?' said Niall, unaware of Liz's thoughts. 'That's Dora all over. Mad as a box of mongeese.'

'Is it mongeese?' asked Irwin, with a frown. 'Or mongooses?'

'Good question,' said Niall. 'Let's look it up.' He took out his phone.

Liz wondered what Dora had wanted. She couldn't explain why she thought it, but she had a feeling she was looking for her.

. . .

AFTER THEY'D LIFTED the dust sheets and washed out the brushes, Liz and Niall headed back to Henrietta Street. To Liz's surprise, she saw her new guests – Mr and Mrs Yarrow – had already arrived at Gull Cottage. Check-in wasn't officially until two o'clock, but luckily she'd done the changeover first thing, and everything was ready for them. She introduced herself, showed them where everything was, and recommended some places they could eat for lunch. Then, after nipping into Kipper to freshen up, she clipped Nelson onto his lead and headed to the Full Moon Café, where she picked up some sandwiches and sausage rolls.

As she was stepping out of the café again, onto Sandgate, Nelson suddenly stopped in his tracks. His hackles went up, and he gave a low growl. Liz looked around, expecting to see Dora Spackle somewhere in the vicinity. The only time Nelson ever growled was when Dora was around – they were sworn enemies. To Liz's surprise, there was no sign of Dora anywhere.

'What's the matter with you, daftie?'

Nelson growled at the shop doorway opposite.

'Come on.' She tugged on his lead. 'We'll be late.'

Liz pulled her hat more firmly onto her head and headed towards the swing bridge, which was the only way to cross the harbour to the west side of town. Luckily the bridge was open, so they were able to cross without waiting. Liz and Nelson hurried, heads down against the rain, past the amusement arcades and fish market on the quayside, and headed up the steps to the West Cliff. The West Cliff was very different to the older, eastern part of the town where Liz lived. Most of the buildings on the esplanade were Edwardian, painted pastel colours, giving the West Cliff all the dignity and elegance of a wealthy spa resort.

Liz and Nelson hurried through the rain to their destination on top of the cliff – a protected glass shelter that looked out over the beach and the grey expanse of the North Sea. It wasn't particularly welcoming today, wind-blown and spattered with salty rain, but for Liz it was a place of refuge and happy memories. She often had lunch there with Kevin Ossett.

Kevin was Benedict's son. He and Liz had been friends long before she and Benedict had started their relationship, and Liz had been worried that it might spoil things. It was still early days, but luckily, it seemed as if it was business as usual. Kevin had responded enthusiastically when she had suggested lunch that morning. She shook the water from her raincoat, sat on the wooden bench and unpacked the sandwiches. From where she sat, she could see the waves crashing on the beach a few hundred yards below. The wide stretch of sand was completely deserted – very different to how it was in the summer, when it was thick with deckchairs and squealing children.

Kevin was late. Liz watched him park his car in the Pavilion car park and hurry to join her in the shelter, his hood pulled up against the rain.

'Blimey,' he gasped, dropping onto the bench beside her. 'Sorry I'm late. Weather's not getting any better, is it?'

'It's hard to believe spring's just around the corner.' Liz poured him coffee from her flask and offered him one of Tilly's sausage rolls. He took it gratefully and rubbed one of Nelson's ears with his free hand. 'I've just almost run over Dora Spackle.'

'Dora?'

'Mm. On the Khyber Pass. She wasn't looking where she was going. In a hurry to get somewhere or other.'

Liz frowned. Dora again. Kevin interrupted her thoughts.

'Sorry,' he said, 'but I'll have to eat and run today.' He

broke off some of his sausage roll and gave it to Nelson. Liz pretended not to see.

'Flint driving you hard?' she asked.

Kevin nodded. 'Something came up just as I was leaving. It's *all hands on deck* at the station.' He grinned. 'Literally.'

'Oh?'

'Anna sent the results through for Daniel Holliday's post-mortem.'

Anna was the assistant coroner and also Kevin's girl-friend. She'd just passed her exams to be able to conduct post-mortems by herself.

Liz shuddered. 'That can't have been a nice one to have as her first solo. Death by drowning.'

Kevin gave her a sideways look.

Liz sat up. 'No? Not death by drowning?'

Kevin took a bite of his sausage roll.

'Come on, Kev, don't be a tease.'

He finished chewing. 'There was no water in his lungs. He also had a head trauma that looks like it happened ante-mortem.'

'*Ante*-mortem? You're saying he was dead when he went in the water?'

'Looks like it.'

'Murder?'

'Suspicious circumstances, at least. We're impounding the *Stella Mae* this afternoon.' He saw her expression and looked alarmed. 'Now, Liz—'

Liz cut him off. 'You don't need to worry. Why should I get involved in this one?'

He gave her a sceptical look.

'Seriously. Why would I? It has nothing to do with me.'

4

'I need your help.' Dora Spackle stood on Liz's doorstep. She had reverted to her usual green cloche hat, which matched her no-nonsense tweed coat and sturdy boots. She glared at Liz from under her umbrella.

'My help?'

Dora nodded. 'I know you don't like me, and I don't like you. But you've helped me before, in a manner of speaking, and I don't have anyone else to turn to.'

'Oh.' Liz blinked, astonished. It was hardly the most persuasive plea for help, but Liz guessed it was probably the best that Dora could manage. 'I suppose you'd better come in, then.'

'Not with that dog of yours. Can you lock him up somewhere?'

'He's not here. Niall's taken him out for a walk.'

Dora cocked her head, listening for proof of Liz's words, then nodded. 'In that case, I'll come in.' She closed her umbrella and stepped inside.

'Let me take your things.'

'No.'

'No?'

'I'm not stopping long.' Dora stood, dripping water onto the kitchen floor. She shook her head when Liz indicated she should take a chair. She hesitated, as if unsure how to begin. Liz decided to help her out.

'Have you been following me, by any chance?' she asked.

'Following you?'

'You were in Neptune Yard this morning, and then on the West Cliff at lunchtime.' She didn't mention Church Street, when Nelson had growled, but suspected that Dora had been there too, hiding in the baker's.

Dora looked affronted. 'Why would I be following you?'

'I thought you might be plucking up the courage to speak to me.'

'It was just a co-incidence. I was just doing what I always do, minding my own business. Something *you* should try occasionally.'

Liz folded her arms. 'If you want my help, Dora, you have a strange way of asking for it.'

Dora had the grace to look slightly ashamed.

Liz realised there was something she needed to say. 'I'm so sorry about Daniel. Such a terrible thing to happen.' She wondered whether Dora knew about the new investigation and decided to play safe by not mentioning it. 'I didn't know you had family in the town,' she said instead.

'He was my sister's boy. She's long gone. He treated my place like a hotel. Whenever he and that wife of his had a row.' Dora's words were sour, but her eyes were reddening.

'Please, Dora, won't you sit down?'

Dora dropped gracelessly onto one of the kitchen chairs. 'Danny was no angel, but he was all I had.'

'I'm sorry.' There was an awkward silence. 'How can I help you?'

Dora put her hand in her pocket and pulled out an envelope, which she passed to Liz. It was just a plain envelope with a name written on it. *Amanda.*

'He gave it to me about a month before he died,' she said. 'Told me to look after it, and if anything happened to him, only to give it to Amanda.'

'Who's Amanda?'

'No idea. But he's been dead nearly a month now, and there's been no sign of her.'

Liz's mind whirled. Why would he give the envelope to Dora? Did he think something might happen to him on the *Stella Mae*? And who was Amanda? She remembered the veiled woman at the funeral. Could she be Amanda?

'Perhaps you should take it to the police?' she said.

'I can't.'

'Why not?'

'He told me not to. Very specifically. I had to give it to Amanda, whoever she is, and no one else. Particularly *not* the police.'

Stranger and stranger. What could possibly be in the envelope that Daniel Holliday didn't want the police to see? Liz looked at the envelope, then back at Dora.

'So what do you want *me* to do?'

'Open it.'

'What?'

'I promised not to.'

They looked at each other. They both knew that would hardly be following the spirit of Daniel's instruction. Liz also knew she shouldn't get involved. But... she had to admit, she was itching to see what was in the envelope. She deflected, buying time.

'Why me?' she asked. 'Of all the people you could have asked to do it, why did you come to me? We don't even like each other.'

Dora had the nerve to look hurt.

'Your words, not mine,' Liz reminded her.

Dora sniffed. 'I suppose that's true. I don't really have friends.' She said it matter-of-factly, with no trace of self-pity. 'But I know you can keep a secret.'

That was true. Liz had many faults, but indiscretion wasn't one of them. During the mysterious affair of Professor Ian Crowby's death the summer before, Liz had discovered things about Dora no one else knew, that could damage Dora's reputation if they became common knowledge. Things she had kept to herself.

Liz turned the envelope over in her hand.

'Do you think we should steam it?' suggested Dora.

Liz shook her head. 'It looks like it'll open easily enough.'

Dora nodded, eager. 'Go on, then.'

Liz hesitated, then slipped her index finger under the flap. It opened without resistance and without tearing. There was a piece of folded paper inside. As Liz pulled it out, something fell to the floor with a clunk. Dora picked it up and held it to the light.

'Looks like a key,' she said.

It *was* a key. Old-fashioned, rusty, and quite small.

'For a padlock of some kind?' suggested Liz.

'Is that all there is?' said Dora.

Liz checked the envelope. 'Looks like it.'

'Is there anything written on the paper?'

Liz turned it over to look at both sides. 'No. It's blank. I imagine Amanda must know what the key is for.'

'So what now?'

'I don't know. We can hardly wander round Whitby trying to fit it into random locks, like a couple of demented Prince Charmings.'

Dora frowned.

'Cinderella,' Liz explained. 'The glass slipper?'

Dora just gave her a sour look. Liz slipped the key and paper back into the envelope and returned it to her.

'So,' said Dora, 'we just have to wait and see if this Amanda person turns up?'

Liz noted the 'we'. She wanted to refute it, but realised that ship had probably sailed. She sighed instead. 'I don't see there's anything else we can do, really.'

'DO YOU KNOW ANYONE called Amanda in the town?'

Tilly frowned, thinking. 'There's old Mandy Salthouse, who used to run the kids' carousel on the pier.'

'How old is she?'

'Must be in her late eighties now, I suppose.'

Liz frowned. Old Mandy Salthouse didn't sound like the kind of person who would have nefarious dealings with Daniel Holliday.

'Why?' asked Tilly, eyes sharp with curiosity.

'No particular reason.'

Tilly's eyes narrowed. She knew Liz better than that.

Liz was saved at that moment by the sudden appearance of Kevin from Benedict's kitchen. 'Tills! Can you put this on the table?' He handed Tilly a huge bowl of nachos and disappeared again. Tilly flashed Liz a look that promised further interrogation. Liz hoped she'd have forgotten about it by the time they were alone again.

Thursday night was mah-jong night, and, as usual, Liz had helped Benedict prepare supper for them to share before the game. Tonight it was Mexican food, and Benedict's house was filled with the enticing aroma of chilli, salsa and home-made guacamole. Benedict lived in a big Edwardian house set back from the road in what was known by locals as the 'posh' part of town, screened by a beech hedge, with glorious views of Pannet Park. The conservatory, where they always ate and played mah-jong, was a proper hothouse, with soaring panes of glass, tropical plants and wicker furniture draped with several cats – a legacy from Benedict's late wife, Katherine.

'Kev!' bellowed Tilly after she'd placed the nachos beside the dips on the table. 'Can you bring some paper towels? It's going to get messy in here otherwise.'

'What did your last servant die of?' shouted Kev from the kitchen. 'Come and get some yourself!'

Tilly headed into the kitchen with a grin. She and Kevin had an easy-going, bantering relationship, more like brother and sister than old school friends.

Liz took a deep breath and looked around the conservatory. It had always been lovely, but the recent addition of fairy lights sprinkled through the vines and larger plants had made it magical. That had been Liz's only contribution so far to Benedict's décor since they'd become a couple. She didn't think she would make any more. Liz hadn't spent the night there yet, and, if she was honest, she wasn't particularly keen to. It still felt very much like Benedict and Katherine's home.

Liz's thoughts were interrupted by the arrival of Benedict, Kevin and Tilly from the kitchen, bearing bowls of chilli, tortilla wraps and kitchen roll. Liz's heart turned over in her chest at the sight of Benedict. His face was rosy from cooking, and he was still handsome – boyish, even – in spite of his fifty-odd years. He made Liz feel like a silly teenager. Benedict caught her looking at him, and winked. She blushed.

'Sit down, everyone,' he said. 'Let's enjoy it while it's hot.'

Liz moved Delilah, the oldest cat in Benedict's menagerie, from her chair to a comfy spot on a wicker sofa so she could sit down. It was quiet for a while after that, with only the scrape of serving spoons and murmurs of appreciation breaking the silence. Liz constructed a tortilla with chilli, lettuce and sour cream and bit into it.

Delicious.

'I bumped into Skipper Masterson this morning.' Benedict was the first to break the appreciative silence. 'Just outside the museum.' Benedict ran the Captain Cook Maritime Museum on Grape Lane.

Tilly grimaced. 'Not a happy bunny, I should think.'

'That's putting it mildly,' said Benedict. 'He's in a sweat about the money he's losing. It's been a week since his boat was impounded.'

Kevin looked unimpressed. 'Can't be helped. As a potential crime scene, forensics need to go over it.'

'Her,' corrected Tilly. 'Boats are always "her", aren't they?'

Benedict nodded. 'They are, traditionally, and have been for hundreds of years. Interestingly, though, Lloyd's Register has recently started to refer to ships as "it".'

'Another victory for the patriarchy,' said Tilly, with a sniff.

As interesting as a detour into feminist waters might be, Liz was keen for them not to change the subject. 'Have you interviewed the crew?' she asked Kevin.

'More than once.' He wiped his mouth on a piece of kitchen paper. 'They all say the same thing. Daniel was sick with a bad stomach. He'd been in and out of the toilet cabin ever since they'd set off from the harbour. Then, when the storm hit, the engine was flooded, and the hull was damaged, and after that, they were all too busy to realise he wasn't on board.'

'So when did they realise?' asked Liz.

'Not until dawn, when the storm had passed. That's when Skipper called us on the ship-to-shore radio.'

Benedict pulled a face. 'That's quite a pretty massive time window.'

'It is,' agreed Kevin. 'Daniel texted Catriona to tell her he was ill before the storm hit, just after midnight. But after that... it's anybody's guess when he went overboard.'

'Not your usual police investigation,' said Benedict.

'Hardly.'

'Someone definitely hit him over the head?' asked Liz.

'We think so,' said Kevin. 'There was major trauma.'

'Maybe something came loose on the boat,' suggested Tilly. 'Hit him and knocked him overboard?'

Liz frowned. 'It would have to have killed him instantly, before he hit the water, or there would have been at least *some* water in his lungs.'

Kevin shook his head. 'That's not what happened.' He popped a nacho into his mouth and spoke around it. 'Whatever hit him hit him more than once.'

'And it was definitely ante-mortem?'

'Definitely.'

Liz thought about that a moment. 'That doesn't necessarily mean it was premeditated,' she said. 'It could have been done in the heat of the moment. Or even an accident.'

'And the killer knew how bad it would look, so just tipped him overboard?' Tilly nodded eagerly. 'I saw something similar on an episode of *Bergerac* once. They were on a yacht.'

'If it happened by accident,' chipped in Kevin, 'he wouldn't have been hit twice.'

Good point.

Liz sipped her wine. 'However it happened,' she said, 'it must have been a shock to have him washing up on Tate Hill beach like that. Really bad luck.'

Kevin lifted an eyebrow. 'Good luck for us, though.'

Liz blushed. 'Of course.'

Benedict gave her a wry look. 'Sometimes, Liz,' he said, 'your ability to embrace your dark side is a little worrying.'

'That's why she's such a good detective,' said Tilly.

'What about me?' said Kevin. 'I'm the actual detective here, remember?'

'You don't have a dark side,' said Tilly. 'Which gives you a different advantage.'

'Does it?' Kevin looked doubtful.

'Mmm.' Tilly nodded. 'It means you're not distracted by your imagination.'

Kevin blinked.

Liz and Benedict exchanged a look. *Ouch.*

'You don't think I have an imagination?' asked Kevin.

Tilly realised she'd slipped up. 'Not a dark one, anyway.'

'Right.' Kevin pulled a face and tackled his chilli, clearly disgruntled.

Liz felt bad for him. He was actually a very good detective – methodical and observant – but in some ways Tilly was right. What made Kevin effective was his adherence to the facts rather than intuition. Completely different to the way she approached things.

LATER, when the game had finished and Kevin and Tilly had gone home, Liz helped Benedict finish tidying.

'Do you think Kevin was upset?'

'About the imagination thing?' asked Benedict. 'Maybe a bit, but he'll get over it.'

'Tilly didn't mean to be rude. She was just being Tilly.'

'He knows her better than anyone. He'll be fine.'

Liz put the last of the glasses in the dishwasher and straightened up. She could hear rain lashing against the kitchen windows behind the shutters.

'Sounds wild out there again.'

'It does,' agreed Benedict. He put his arms around her from behind. 'You don't have to go if you don't want to.' He kissed her neck. 'You could stay here.'

Liz froze. 'I don't think so.'

He stopped kissing her.

'Nelson,' she said, by way of explanation.

'Niall's there. You could text him, ask him to take Nelson out. I'm sure he won't mind.'

Liz knew he was right. Niall wouldn't mind a bit. But...

She turned to face him. 'I don't have any of my toiletries or anything. I think I'd rather go home, if you don't mind.'

Benedict gave her a squeeze. 'If that's what you want, of course I don't mind.'

Liz watched his lips as he said it. Benedict had a tell that she'd come to recognise during their many evenings playing mah-jong together. Whenever he bluffed or told a lie, the left-hand corner of his mouth would twitch. It was a dead give-away, and one he was entirely unable to control, even though she'd warned him about it. As he spoke, the left side of his mouth flickered, almost imperceptibly. Liz's heart sank. At some point, she was going to have to get over her reluctance to stay in Katherine's house.

But not tonight.

5

'You want them filleted or just as they come?' Lesley Howson had to raise her voice to be heard over the chatter of customers in her fishmonger's shop on Baxtergate. The building had been a fishmonger for generations and was decorated with Victorian tiles showing scenes of Whitby, most of them fishing related. The shop was always popular, but was particularly busy that morning because Friday was the traditional day to eat fish.

'Filleted, please,' said Liz. Neither she nor Niall enjoyed picking the bones out, and her own filleting skills were lamentable.

She'd decided on plaice for dinner, but it hadn't been an easy choice. There was a bewildering array of fish to choose from – massive codling, sea bream, sea bass, herrings and eels, all displayed on ice with prices. There were shellfish, too: slippery grey prawns piled on trays waiting to be scooped into bags, scallops, cockles and mussels, a dozen crabs and even a few lobsters, their claws taped and waving in protest. The only thing that was missing was mackerel, but that was only because it wasn't mackerel season.

Liz had been surprised to see how well stocked the shop was, considering the *Stella Mae* was still out of operation. She supposed Mike had found a supplier outside the town – Scarborough, Bridlington or even Grimsby – to make up the deficit.

'Mike! I'm run off my feet out here!' Lesley called into the back room. 'Can you come and fillet these?'

Mike emerged and spotted Liz. He wiped his hands on his white overall, leaving pinkish smears. 'Morning, Mrs Mac.' He looked quite different in his starched hat and rubber boots than he did when he was doing his deliveries in his high-vis gear. He took Liz's plaice from Lesley and slapped them expertly onto the filleting slab.

'How are things with you?' he asked, flashing his knife through the fish like a professional assassin.

'Great, thanks.' Liz tore her fascinated gaze from the blade. 'How's Billy?'

Mike rolled his eyes. 'Bored. And broke. Not the best combination.'

'Hopefully the police will release the *Stella Mae* soon.'

'Hopefully.' Mike tossed the bones and skin into the waste bin under the counter and wrapped the two fillets in waxed paper. 'The devil finds work for idle hands.'

'Could be worse, though.' She looked at him meaningfully. 'Much worse.'

It took him a moment to get it. 'Like Doc, you mean?'

She nodded.

'I suppose.' He sighed. 'But even though the bugger's gone, he's still causing problems.' He saw the look on Liz's face and backtracked. 'Sorry,' he said. 'Things are tricky at the moment. Best not speak ill of the dead, eh?' He gave her the fishy package. 'Is there anything else I can get you?'

Outside, Liz saw that Billy and Potsy Potter were sitting on the shop windowsill. Billy was busy on his phone, but Potsy beamed when he spotted her.

'Mrs Mac!' He looked eagerly at the pavement, then frowned. 'No Nelson today?' He and Nelson were great friends.

'No, I left him snoring at home.'

'Maybe I can take him for a walk some time?' He blinked at her through the lenses of his thick spectacles.

'Why not? Just knock on the door when you're passing.'

'Excellent!' He beamed. 'Will do!'

Liz didn't think he would. Even though Potsy was in his early forties, there was something childlike about him. He wore brightly patterned sweaters, too-short trousers, and was full of fleeting enthusiasms that had included skateboarding, marathon running, and Motocross. He had even briefly owned a dirt bike, even though he couldn't ride one. Some unkind people in the town – mostly the same people who called Nelson the ugliest dog in Yorkshire – liked to dismiss him as simple-minded. Liz didn't think he was. She thought he just saw the world in a slightly different way to most people. She knew she could trust him with Nelson. They would look after each other.

'How are you, Billy?' she asked the man beside Potsy.

Billy looked up reluctantly from his phone, dragging his eyes from the screen. 'Right enough, I suppose.' Billy was a well-built lad, with the outdoorsy, raw-boned good looks of a farmer. He slipped the phone into his pocket and shrugged. 'I just wish I could get back to work.'

Something tugged briefly at Liz's attention, but slid away again before she could grasp it.

She nodded at Billy. 'I'll keep my fingers crossed the *Stella Mae*'s back in action soon.'

. . .

IT WAS ONLY THAT EVENING, when she and Niall were eating the plaice (with parsley potatoes and lemon) that she realised what her subconscious revelation had been.

'Did you swallow a bone or something?' asked Niall, having spotted the odd look on her face.

Liz shook her head. 'I'm fine. But I need to make a phone call when we're done.'

Niall finished his last mouthful. 'That was grand. Why don't you go and make your call, and I'll tidy up here?'

Liz took her phone upstairs to the sitting room.

Kevin picked up straightaway. 'Liz.'

'Are you still at work?'

'Unfortunately.'

'Is it okay to talk for a minute? I have a quick question for you.'

'Oh?' Kevin's voice turned wary.

'Was Daniel Holliday's phone on him when he was found?'

'Why?'

'I'm just interested.'

'No. It wasn't. We haven't found it on the *Stella Mae* yet either.'

'He definitely called his wife while he was on board?'

'He texted her.'

'You're sure?'

'Of course I'm sure. I've seen the text. And the phone mast at Grimsby confirmed it.' Kevin sniffed. 'I might not have an *imagination*, but I know how to do my job.'

'You do realise Tilly didn't mean that the way it came out?'

'Whatever,' said Kevin, dismissively. 'What's your gripe about the phone?'

'The oilskins had pockets, I assume?'

'Zipped ones.'

'So why isn't his phone in one of them? Who would have a phone in their hand on deck in that weather?'

Kevin was silent while he thought about that. 'Good point. You think someone tossed it overboard?'

'If it's not somewhere on the boat, that's the only scenario that makes sense. It certainly confirms the murder theory, doesn't it?'

'I suppose.' Kevin's voice took on a warning note. 'I know you can't help being interested... that *imagination* of yours... but I have to ask, you don't have any particular reason to get involved in this investigation, do you?'

'None at all,' said Liz, a little too quickly. Dora Spackle's mystery with the key was only tangentially connected. 'I'm just trying to be helpful.'

'Okay. Good.'

'Can I ask, have any of the trawlermen ever been in trouble with the police?'

'Now you're just being nosy.'

'Trying to be helpful, like I said.'

Kevin sighed. 'Just one. Christian Petit. He's new to the crew, only been there a few months. When we ran a check, we found out he's done time in France for theft.'

'Do you think Masterson knows that?'

'Doubt it. I can't imagine Petit volunteered that information, and I can't imagine the skipper would have taken him on if he had.'

'Interesting.'

'Everyone on the crew is a suspect. Problem is, at the moment we have no way of ruling *any* of them out.'

THE NEXT MORNING, Liz popped into Gull Cottage to check on the Yarrows. They were there for a full fortnight, but seemed to be enjoying themselves in spite of the weather.

'It's nothing we're not used to,' said Donna Yarrow, a small woman with iron-grey curls. 'Is it, Jack?'

Her husband looked up from his *Sea Angler* magazine. 'Home from home.'

'You sure there's nothing else you need?'

'We're fine, thanks. We're just wondering what to do with ourselves today.'

'Have you been to the Captain Cook Museum yet?' asked Liz. Captain James Cook, the famous eighteenth-century explorer, was one of North Yorkshire's most famous sons.

Donna shook her head. 'We haven't got round to that yet, have we, Jack?'

'I can recommend it,' continued Liz. 'It has some really interesting exhibits – models of ships and maps of Cook's travels – and the building is fascinating, too. And' – she produced her final rabbit from the hat – 'there's a fantastic craft beer shop just around the corner.'

Jack Yarrow grinned, revealing a row of gappy teeth. 'Now you're talking.'

After she left Gull Cottage, Liz collected Nelson and her laptop and headed to the café, where she'd promised Iris she would give her a hand to renew her bus pass online. She'd offered to go up to the Anchorage to help her, but Iris, who liked to get out and about, had insisted on meeting her at the Full Moon.

Iris wasn't there when Liz arrived, but the café was busy, packed with people taking refuge from the blustery weather. Liz managed to find a free table and unclipped Nelson, who made a beeline for the squeaky pig Mags kept for him behind the counter. Tilly emerged through the beaded curtains with a laden tray and spotted her.

'With you in a minute, Liz.' She headed to one of the bigger tables to deliver her burden of food and drink.

Liz took off her wet coat and hat and hung them on the

back of her chair, then retrieved her laptop from her bag and switched it on. By the time Tilly returned to take her order, she was just starting to warm through.

'You're busy this morning,' she said.

'We are.' Tilly frowned. 'And we're short-handed too. Gryzna hasn't turned up.'

'Really?' That wasn't like Gryzna.

'No phone call or anything.'

Liz was worried. 'Maybe one of the boys is ill?'

'Maybe. It must be something serious, to leave us high and dry like this. Mags is trying to track her down. What can I get you?'

'A cheese and onion toastie would be lovely. And tea, of course.'

'Of course.' Tilly grinned. 'What would a toastie be without tea?'

The bell on the door tinkled, and the whirlwind that was Iris Gladwell barged in, wearing a see-through plastic rain hood and a Barbour overcoat that almost reached the floor. She spotted Liz and marched to her table while Dickie shook out their umbrella in the doorway.

'GREAT WEATHER FOR DUCKS.' Iris wrestled her coat off, almost elbowing the woman on the next table in the head as she did so. She gave her coat a vigorous shake, splashing water everywhere, then thrust it at Tilly to hang it up for her.

'TWO SCONES, PLEASE, AND TEA.'

'You want jam with them?'

Iris looked at Tilly as if she were mad. 'ON A SATUR-DAY? NO, THANK YOU VERY MUCH!' She had very specific, unfathomable, and ever-changing rules about when she would and wouldn't eat jam.

'Actually,' said Dickie, mildly. 'I'd like a coffee, not tea. Black, please.' He squeezed his spare jockey's frame onto a vacant seat beside Iris.

'Black coffee it is. Coming right up.' Tilly headed back to the kitchen. She'd almost made it to the beaded curtain when Mags appeared through it. There was an odd look on her face.

Tilly frowned. 'Are you alright, love? You look like you've seen a ghost.'

Mags shook her head. 'It's Gryzna.' She paused to gather her thoughts and choose the right words. 'Apparently... according to her neighbour... she's been taken into custody.'

'What did she say?' asked Dickie, leaning forward. 'I didn't quite catch that.'

Iris turned to him, eyes round. 'GRYZNA'S BEEN ARRESTED.'

6

'I'm not sure *arrested* is really the right word,' said Mags, doubtfully.

'I DON'T KNOW WHAT ELSE YOU WOULD CALL IT WHEN YOU LOCK SOMEONE UP.'

They were all sitting around the table in Benedict's conservatory, the only venue big enough to accommodate all of Gryzna's friends.

'I don't understand,' said Irwin. 'Wasn't she supposed to have a hearing?'

'That's what I thought.' Tilly nodded. 'Some time soon, wasn't it?'

'April,' said Liz. 'I'm sure she said April.'

'Where is she exactly?' asked Benedict. 'Does anyone know?'

Everyone looked at Kevin, who shrugged. 'I have no idea. The immigration service has nothing to do with us. They're a law unto themselves, quite literally.'

'What about the boys?' asked Mags. 'Her neighbour said they were taken at the same time. Are they with her?'

Kevin shrugged again. 'I don't know.'

Niall groaned. 'This is terrible. Gryzna must be doing her *nut.*'

Liz almost smiled. Gryzna wasn't the kind of person to take any kind of nonsense lying down.

'She *is* in the country illegally,' Irwin reminded them.

'Escaping from a brutal regime,' said Liz.

Everyone stared at her. That wasn't common knowledge, even among Gryzna's friends.

'Poor Lukasz and Eryk,' said Mags. 'They don't even speak Polish.'

'Actually,' said Liz, 'Gryzna comes from Belarus.'

That was also news to everyone else. Benedict was the first to break the surprised silence. 'I don't imagine the boys will be an issue.'

Tilly was appalled. 'Surely they won't deport Gryzna on her own? They won't split them up?'

'I'm afraid it's a possibility.'

'What did he say?' asked Dickie.

'THEY'RE GOING TO TAKE THE BOYS AWAY FROM GRYZNA, PUT THEM IN AN ORPHANAGE AND SEND HER OUT OF THE COUNTRY.'

'I didn't say that.' Benedict hurried to correct Iris. 'But I think we should prepare ourselves that things might not work out the way we want them to.'

'She'll get Legal Aid, won't she?' queried Mags.

Benedict ran a hand through his hair. 'I doubt it.'

'Isn't there anything we can do?' asked Liz.

'I have a friend who's a barrister,' said Benedict. 'I'm sure he'll be able to put me in touch with someone who knows immigration. But it probably won't be cheap.'

'Whatever it takes,' said Mags. She looked around the little group. A warm wave of affection washed over Liz when everyone nodded. Not many of them had much money, but there was no question of not helping Gryzna if they could.

'In the meantime,' she suggested, 'shouldn't we try to find out exactly where Gryzna and the boys are?'

'I'll do it,' said Kevin. 'I have some contacts in social services.'

Benedict nodded. 'In the meantime, let's see if we can get her decent legal representation. Then we'll take it from there.'

When everyone else had gone, Benedict took Liz in his arms.

'Are you okay?' he asked.

'Not really. It's just too awful to think about Gryzna being sent away. Being split up from the boys.'

'I know.' He kissed her forehead. 'Wherever she is, she'll be worried sick.'

'You really think she won't qualify for Legal Aid?'

'It isn't easy to get these days. If it comes to it, I'll foot the legal bill. I can afford it.'

'You're a good man, Benedict Ossett.'

'A lucky one.' He gave her a squeeze. 'A very, very lucky one.'

LIZ HEADED home to let Benedict make his calls. It had finally stopped raining, so she took a detour to stretch her legs, up through the maze-like Victorian streets of the town and onto the West Cliff, to the whale-bone arch. The arch was a well-known Whitby landmark – the jawbone of a mighty whale that had been erected as a memorial to all the whalers in the town who had died at sea. The bone had been replaced at some point by a resin replica, but it still framed the gaunt ruins of the abbey on the opposite side of the harbour beautifully.

Liz took a deep breath, looked at the view, and tried very hard not to think about Gryzna. There was nothing she could do at that moment to help her, so she determined she should reserve all her anger and indignation for the moment when there was.

The sky was still grey, with the promise of more rain to come. Seagulls wheeled and yodelled overhead, more numerous than usual, driven inland by the bad weather. Although the wind had dropped quite a bit, it still sliced through her padded jacket, making her shiver. She decided she should keep moving.

Making her way down the winding road to the quayside, she saw that the *Stella Mae* was still in dock. Yellow crime tape fluttered on her decks, and there was a cordon at the top of the ladder, where a single police officer kept guard. As she got closer, she recognised PC Bill Williams, his long face even more woeful than usual. He managed a weak smile when he saw her.

'Mrs Mac.'

'Are you okay?' she asked. 'You look frozen stiff.'

'I was supposed to be relieved an hour ago. I think DI Flint's forgotten about me.' He shuffled from foot to foot in an attempt to keep warm.

'Haven't you radioed?'

'I have, but...' He didn't finish his sentence: they both knew Flint wasn't subject to the rules of ordinary mortals.

'Can I get you a coffee or something?'

'Could you?' He stretched his frozen features into a smile. 'I'd have got some myself, but didn't want to leave my post.'

She went to the coffee kiosk beside the fish market and bought two large lattes and two donuts, then took them back to the cordon on the quayside. Williams wrapped his numb fingers gratefully around the polystyrene cup and took a sip. She waited until his teeth had stopped chattering before engaging him in conversation.

'Strange business,' she said, nodding down at the *Stella Mae*.

'You can say that again.'

'What do you think happened?' She knew that Williams, affable and awkward, was often the butt of jokes at the station, but also that he was a lot sharper than anyone gave him credit for.

Williams took a bite of donut and chewed it thoughtfully before answering. 'Flint's sure she's going to catch a killer, but I think she's barking up the wrong tree.'

She prodded him again. 'What do you think happened?'

'The obvious. Doc slipped on deck, hit his head on something a couple of times in the swell, and then washed overboard. I know all the crew except the Frenchman, and I don't think any of them are capable of killing someone. Even Doc.'

'He wasn't well liked?' Liz knew the answer to that, but wanted to get Williams's take on Daniel Holliday.

He pulled a face. 'I know I shouldn't speak ill of the dead, Mrs Mac, but... let's just say he was never going to win citizen of the year.'

'Why not?'

The constable finished his donut and licked the sugar off his frozen fingers. 'He went out with my sister, Becky, for a while, back when they were both in school. Used to mess her around something rotten.'

Liz frowned. 'You don't mean...?'

'No. He never hit her. But he two-timed her. Three-timed her, in fact. When she found out, she confronted him in our kitchen. Dad chucked him out. Broke Becky's heart.' Williams shrugged. 'She's married now, with twins, so... all's well that ends well.'

'Except for Doc.'

'Except for Doc.'

'Do you think he changed?'

'Nah.' Williams shook his head. 'A leopard doesn't change his spots.'

Liz wasn't sure she agreed. In her experience, people often got better as they got older. It was appalling to think that anyone's personality should be set in stone in adolescence. The world would be a *terrible* place.

She finished her latte and dumped her empty cup in the bin on the quayside beside them. 'I should be getting on.'

'Thanks, Mrs Mac.' Williams saluted her with his cup. 'You saved my life.'

Liz grinned at him. 'Anytime.'

SHE SPENT the rest of the day quietly in Kipper Cottage, planning the refurbishment of Benbow Cottage. Niall was out, working a shift behind the bar at the Duke of York – he did that whenever he could to supplement his income as a student – so she had the place to herself. She worked on her laptop on the table in the kitchen, trawling furniture websites and making notes while Nelson snored at her feet.

It wasn't easy to furnish a cottage for a holiday let. It had to be homely and welcoming, with enough character to make it stand out from the competition, but not so much it would be seen as eccentric and put people off. There wasn't much of Iris's furniture that could be used, as she'd taken the best of it to furnish her room at the Anchorage. The cottage needed a double bed – modern and brand new was usually best for beds – plus a table and chairs, a wardrobe and a couple of comfy chairs. Liz decided leather would be best for the chairs, as it was easy to keep clean, hard-wearing, and – if she managed to track down vintage ones – characterful enough for a fisherman's cottage. But, having looked through some online sites, she was appalled by how much vintage leather armchairs could cost, even the most battered ones. She doubted she'd find cheaper in the antique shops in the town either – they were geared more to tourists than locals and were often pricey. Maybe a visit to the auction rooms in Kirkbymoorside would be a good idea? She took a look at their website to see when there were viewings.

Kevin called just after three, to tell her he'd managed to track down Gryzna's boys, who were in a temporary foster home in Middlesbrough. He still hadn't found out where Gryzna was.

Benedict called just a few minutes later, with news that he'd managed to find a lawyer who could help them. Caroline Burlington worked for a large law firm in York that specialised in immigration applications and appeals. He'd only managed to talk with her for a few minutes on the phone, but she'd told him that the boys would get automatic citizenship, as they had been in the country more than ten years. But Gryzna was a different matter. She would only be able to appeal her deportation on the basis of her relation to the boys if she could prove her separation was 'unduly harsh'.

Liz was incensed. 'Surely any separation of a mother from her children is unduly harsh.'

'Not in the eyes of the Home Office.' Benedict's voice on the other end of the phone was bleak.

'That's outrageous! How on earth can you "prove" such a thing?'

'Expert reports, apparently.'

'What does that involve?'

'I don't know yet. I've arranged a proper meeting with Caroline on Thursday. I should call the others and let them know what's happening. See you later, sweetheart.'

'Later.' She hung up.

Neither of them had used the L word yet. As close as they were, Liz thought they were still some way off that. If she was honest, she couldn't imagine using the word 'love' to anyone but her dead husband, Mark.

After Kevin's and Benedict's calls, Liz found it difficult to concentrate on what she'd been doing. It seemed frivolous and uncaring to be thinking about leather armchairs and antique auctions when Gryzna was sitting somewhere, alone and frantic, and the boys were in a strange house with strange people, not understanding what was happening to them. How on earth was anyone supposed to 'prove' their separation was 'unduly harsh'? It was patently clear that it would be, to anyone with a heart.

Nelson sat up and pricked his ears.

Liz eyed him. 'What?'

He growled, low in his throat, and glared at the front door.

Someone knocked.

Yip, yip, yip!

Nelson leapt up and shot to the door like a furry guided missile. Liz had to use all her strength to pull him away. She managed to manhandle him into the understairs cupboard, and locked it. The door shuddered as he hurled himself against it, snarling and yipping.

Liz straightened her clothes and opened the door.

'Dora, what can I do for you?'

As Liz expected, the museum curator stood on the doorstep, but for once she didn't seem to care about Nelson's whereabouts. She twisted her hands, distraught.

'You have to come,' she said. 'I've been burgled!'

7

'Is there anything missing?' asked Liz.

'I don't know. I can't tell, in this mess.' Dora looked sorrowfully around her brown 1970s-style kitchen. Every drawer had been emptied, every cupboard ransacked.

'How did they get in?'

'A key. Under the mat outside.'

Almost everyone in the town kept a key somewhere outside, under a plant pot or in a window box, or, if it was a holiday let, in a key safe on the wall. The doormat was a bit obvious, though.

'I don't understand why you won't call the police.'

'It's none of their ruddy business, that's why.'

Liz looked at Dora. She really was as stubborn as a mule. 'What's it like in the rest of the house?'

'Just the same. Come and see.' Dora led Liz down a narrow passageway that opened into the lounge. Liz gasped, not at the state of the room, which was just as bad as the kitchen, but at the view. The full vista of Whitby harbour spread out before them through the window like a movie in Cinemascope. Dora's cottage, Anchor Cottage, was in New

Way Ghaut, a narrow passageway that ran parallel to Church Street. Liz had only visited it once, the autumn before, but that visit had been confined to the kitchen. She'd never imagined the splendour of the view from the lounge. It almost made up for Dora's taste in furnishings, which were ubiquitously brown and seemed to be stuck somewhere in the late 1970s.

'What a mess.' Dora sighed. 'It's going to take hours to put straight.'

Just like the kitchen, the contents of every cupboard had been strewn around the room like confetti. Books, ornaments, magazines. Liz noted, however, that no real damage had been done – no soft furnishings ripped, nothing smashed. Dora's bulgy portable TV still sat on the dresser. Maybe the thieves hadn't taken it because it was so old-fashioned?

'Where do you keep your valuables?'

'Valuables!' Dora scoffed. 'There's only my grandmother's necklace.'

Liz knew the necklace well. It was only thanks to her that it was back in Dora's possession.

'Has it gone?'

'No, it's still where I left it, in my jewellery box in the bedroom.'

Stranger and stranger. But then a thought occurred to Liz. 'Where's the key? The envelope and the key Daniel left you?'

'In my handbag. I had it out with me.' Understanding dawned on Dora's face. 'Do you think that was what they were after?'

Liz shrugged. 'It's possible.'

'Amanda!'

'I doubt it. Why would Amanda, whoever she is, go to the trouble of breaking into your house when she could just knock on your door and ask for the envelope? Did anyone else know that Daniel gave you it?'

'Only you.' Dora's eyes narrowed with suspicion.

'For God's sake, Dora, *I* didn't do it! What would I want with it? I don't even know what it's for.'

Dora sniffed. 'Do you want a cup of tea?'

Liz realised that was an apology. She wondered why Dora had come to her for help, then remembered that Dora had no friends. Liz was probably the nearest thing she had to a confidante, which was sad.

'So sorry, Dora, but I can't stay.' She made an effort to soften her refusal. 'I have to get back to Nelson.' She'd let him out of the cupboard before she'd left Kipper, but guessed he wouldn't be able to settle properly, knowing she'd disappeared in the company of his nemesis.

Dora glowered and followed Liz back to the kitchen.

'Keep the key safe,' urged Liz. 'On you if possible.'

Dora looked appalled. 'I can't keep it.'

'What?'

Dora grabbed her handbag from the table and rummaged in it. She thrust Daniel's envelope at Liz.

'You take it.'

'I don't want it.'

'I won't sleep a wink. What if they come back for it?'

'If they're going to come back, they'll do it even if the key's not here, won't they?'

'I don't care.' Dora was immune to Liz's logic. 'I don't want it here.' She thrust the envelope at Liz and then said a word Liz never thought to hear from her lips. 'Please.'

Liz weakened. 'What if Amanda comes?'

'I'll send her to you.'

Great. But Liz knew she was fighting a losing battle. That one word – *please* – had undone her. She took the envelope from Dora, who relaxed visibly as soon as it was out of her hands.

Dora saw Liz out. As Liz was heading up the path, she called out after her, 'Don't do anything stupid with it!'

WHEN SHE GOT BACK to Kipper Cottage, Liz was relieved to see that Niall was home from the Duke. He was chopping onions, wearing her apron, with a wad of tissue paper stuffed up each nostril.

'I thought I'd make us something Italian tonight,' he said nasally, through his two-ply protection.

Liz's heart sank. 'Actually, I'm going to Benedict's. Sorry, I forgot to tell you.'

'Oh.' Niall did his best not to look disappointed. 'No worries. More for us, eh, Nelson?'

Nelson wagged his tail. Niall was under strict instructions not to feed him human food, but by Nelson's enraptured attention, Liz guessed that something had already found its way 'accidentally' onto the floor.

'There's a message for you on the answerphone,' said Niall.

Liz made a mental note to listen to it, but went upstairs first to her bedroom and put the envelope and key under her mattress. It seemed a bit dramatic – whoever had broken into Dora's would have no reason to think she'd given the key to her – but Liz supposed a bit of caution couldn't hurt.

She went down to the sitting room to pick up the message from the answerphone. As Niall had said, the red light was blinking. Liz pressed the button.

'Hello. This is Finnegan Harewood from the Department of Social Services in Middlesbrough. I'm trying to reach Mrs Elizabeth McLuckie. Could you please call me back on 01642 100111. There is something urgent I wish to discuss with you.'

. . .

'THEY WANT me to take the boys.'

'Really?' Benedict's eyes widened.

'They set fire to the shed in their foster home, then somehow managed to persuade social services they'd behave themselves with me.'

'What about Gryzna? Does she know?'

'They say she's delighted with the idea.'

Benedict nodded. 'She would be. It's so much better to have Eryk and Lukasz with you than someone they don't know.'

Liz was flattered the boys had thought of her. She and Mark had never had children, thanks to a virulent dose of mumps Mark had caught as a teenager. After considering adoption, they had eventually decided against it – they were content enough with each other. Liz's maternal urges had naturally been suppressed when Mark was alive, but had resurrected in recent years as an impulse to take younger people under her wing. Niall was a good example – she had scooped him up after he'd been fired from the museum the summer before, given him a roof over his head, and even engineered him another job by blackmailing Dora for a reference. But that was another story...

The Polonsky boys were a different kettle of fish. They could be a handful at the best of times – not maliciously naughty, but full of restless energy and curiosity. They'd be a huge, unlooked-for responsibility.

Benedict was trying to read her thoughts on her face. 'What are you going to say?'

'Yes, of course.' There was no question in Liz's mind. In spite of all her misgivings, she couldn't bear the thought of the boys on their own in a strange town with strange people, not knowing what was happening to their mum. 'I'll have to move back into Gull, though.' Gull Cottage had one more bedroom than Kipper – a twin room, perfect for the boys. 'I'll have to ask the Yarrows if they mind moving for their last few days.'

'There is another solution,' said Benedict. His eyes were warm on hers.

Liz frowned. She could guess what was coming, and dreaded it.

He pressed on regardless. 'You could come here. You and the boys. I have plenty of room.'

That was true. Benedict's big house had many bedrooms and a garden – more than enough space for the boys to run about in. But... Liz really didn't want to move in. She wanted their relationship to progress naturally, without external pressure. And she wasn't sure she could live in Katherine's house.

She hesitated, knowing an outright refusal would hurt him.

'I'm not sure,' she said instead. 'Why don't we see how it goes?'

ONCE LIZ HAD EXPLAINED everything to the Yarrows the next morning, they were more than happy to move.

'Of course we don't mind.' Donna patted her on the hand. 'We're only here for another few days anyway.'

'You don't have to worry about the changeover,' said Liz, anxious not to inconvenience them too much. 'Just go for lunch, and it'll all be done by the time you get back.'

That turned out to be optimistic. When Donna and Jack returned from their lengthy feast in the famous Magpie Café, quite a few of Liz's and Niall's things – Niall's books and the suitcases with their clothes in – were still on the pavement. Liz, Niall and Benedict were all red-faced with exertion.

'I'm so sorry,' said Liz when she saw Jack and Donna at the door. 'I thought we'd be done by now.'

'Don't be daft,' said Donna. 'We'll give you a hand with the last of it, won't we, Jack?'

'No worries.' The big lifeboat man picked up one of the suitcases as if it were a feather and carried it into Gull Cottage.

In less than a half hour, the changeover was complete, and the Yarrows were making themselves comfortable in front of the fire in Kipper's sitting room.

'Are you sure there's nothing else you need?' asked Liz. She really hoped their enforced move hadn't spoiled their holiday.

'We're fine,' Donna assured her. 'Snug as bugs in rugs.'

Jack spotted Liz's copy of the *Whitby Bugle* on the table and picked it up.

LOCAL TRAWLER IMPOUNDED AFTER FATAL TRAGEDY.

'Terrible business,' he said.

'We've heard all about it,' added Donna. 'People can talk of little else in the shops and restaurants.'

Jack tutted. 'Boats lose crew like that more often than people think. But at least they weren't too far out, and his family got the lad home again.'

Liz frowned. 'They were quite a way out, I think.'

'I doubt it.' Jack saw Liz's puzzled look. 'He washed up on the beach here, in the harbour, didn't he?'

Liz nodded.

'Then they must have been pretty close to shore. A couple of miles out at the most.'

'Really?' Liz frowned. That was odd. Very odd.

She left the Yarrows and found Benedict in Gull Cottage, putting away the last of her groceries.

'Do you know anything about tides?' she asked him.

'A bit. But I wasn't a navigator. Why?' He reached up to stack the tinned tomatoes on the top shelf of the cupboard.

'Jack Yarrow reckons Daniel Holliday couldn't have washed up on the beach here if the *Stella Mae* was properly out at sea.'

'Maybe they didn't get far? Maybe he went overboard early in the trip?'

'But he texted his wife at midnight. Surely, they would have been quite a way out by then?'

'I suppose it depends what time they left the harbour.'

'I suppose.'

'Do you want the dog food in this cupboard, or shall I put it under the stairs?'

'Um... under the cupboard, please.' She answered Benedict's question distractedly. Why had Daniel Holliday washed up on Tate Hill beach when he should, by rights, still be adrift somewhere in the North Sea?

8

Early the next morning, Liz was giving the kitchen in Gull one last preparatory scrub ready for Eryk and Lukasz's arrival when she heard whistling outside in the street. 'The Girl from Ipanema'. She opened the door quickly and caught Mike Howson by surprise.

'Hello!' he said, bringing his herring trolley to a halt. 'I wasn't expecting to see you there.'

'I've moved in here because it's bigger. I'm going to be looking after the Polonsky boys.'

'Good luck with that.' Mike pulled a face. He'd had more than a few run-ins with Eryk and Lukasz in the past.

'Fancy a cuppa when you've dropped those off?'

'Love to, but I don't have time this morning. I've promised Earl I'd help him take some of Doc's stuff to the Mission.'

'How's Catriona?'

'She's managing, I think. But she's a quiet lass. Always has been. It's hard to know what's really going on in her head. And grief's a funny thing.'

'It is.' Liz knew that better than most.

'None of her family were happy when she married him.

Earl in particular. He told Doc he'd come after him if he ever hurt her. Now the lad's dead, though, Earl doesn't know how to handle it.'

'It must be difficult.'

Mike scratched his head. 'It's just a bad business all round.' He caught sight of movement in the doorway of the smokehouse. Someone waiting for him.

'Got to dash.'

A thought occurred to her. 'Do you know if your Billy's around this morning?'

'I doubt it. He doesn't get out of his pit these days until after lunch. Why do you ask?'

'I need a quick word.' She hoped she wouldn't have to explain what that word was. Luckily, Mike was in a hurry and didn't demand further explanation.

Liz went thoughtfully back into Gull Cottage. The boys were due to arrive at eleven. If Billy wasn't around until lunchtime, she'd have to wait until another day to ask him exactly where the *Stella Mae* had been at midnight on the night of the storm.

She had to go to the supermarket first, anyway. She tried to think what kind of food Eryk and Lukasz liked, but could only really come up with hotdogs, which was what they usually ordered at the Full Moon. Hotdogs it would have to be, at least until she could ask the boys in person. She would get some donuts, too. All boys liked donuts, and she was sure a sweet treat would be appreciated after their ordeal in Middlesbrough.

The supermarket was surprisingly busy for so early in the week. It was almost ten o'clock by the time she'd packed her bags at the checkout and hurried out onto New Quay Plaza. She wanted to get home and unpacked before the boys arrived.

She glanced up and was surprised to see someone she

recognised coming out of one of the modern flats on the other side of the road. She couldn't believe her luck.

'BILLY!' Liz called out to him. She couldn't wave because of her shopping bags.

He threw a quick look over his shoulder, but before she could acknowledge him or make a move towards him, he put his head down and hurried off along the quayside. Liz stopped in her tracks, bewildered. Perhaps he hadn't heard her? Or hadn't recognised her? Then she saw a pale face at the window of the flat he'd come out of. Catriona Holliday spotted her and moved quickly out of sight.

Liz was puzzled. Mike had said Billy hadn't been getting out of his bed until noon, so what was he doing at Catriona's? And why had he skulked off so quickly? He had acted very suspiciously – guiltily, even. But guilty of what? There was an obvious conclusion to jump to, but Liz resisted it. Doc had only been dead a few weeks. Surely not?

All lingering questions about Catriona Holliday's love life vanished with the arrival of Finnegan Harewood and the boys, bang on the dot of eleven.

'Isn't there anywhere to park?' was the first thing the lanky, stiff-faced social worker said when she answered the door. His Ford Focus was blocking the street.

'Sorry, no, you'll have to go to the end of the street and turn around. The nearest car park is on the other side of Church Street.'

Lukasz and Eryk blinked solemnly at her from the back of the car. They didn't look any the worse for their ordeal, except their usually spiky hair had been combed flat. They looked bizarrely tamed.

'Never mind,' said Harewood, briskly. 'I'll call you later to go through our checklist.' He opened the back door, which, Liz realised, must have had child locks. The boys scrambled out and rushed past Liz into the cottage. Harewood retrieved their luggage from the boot.

'Is this all they have?' asked Liz. There was only one sports holdall.

'I believe so,' said Harewood. 'The intervention was pretty swift.'

Intervention. Liz's lip curled. Harewood saw it, but chose to ignore it.

'I'll call you this afternoon.' There was a distinct look of relief on his face as he got back into his car. Liz slammed the door shut before he drove off.

'What was Nelson doing in the cupboard?' demanded Eryk. The boys were petting Nelson, who was putting up with it bravely, wincing under their enthusiastic administrations.

'He barks too much when there's someone at the door.' That had only been the case since he'd last heard Dora there. Liz supposed he'd get over it.

'How are you both?' she asked, scanning their faces.

Lukasz lifted his chin. 'Where's Mum?'

'I don't know.' Liz knew the boys had built-in BS detectors, so decided that honesty was the best policy. 'Kevin's trying to find out. Didn't they say anything to you?'

'Not a thing. And they locked us up.'

'They didn't.'

'They *practically* did. We weren't allowed to watch telly, and they made us shower *twice a day.*'

'*Twice a day!*' echoed Eryk, outraged.

'That's awful.'

'It's child abuse, that's what it is.' Lukasz sniffed. 'I'm going to get Kevin to arrest them.'

Liz thought a change of subject was in order. She nodded at the sports bag. 'Is this all you have?'

Lukasz nodded grimly. 'They made us go naked.'

Liz gave him a disbelieving look.

'*Practically* naked.' *Practically* was clearly his new favourite word. 'They didn't let us choose our own clothes. All we had was one pair of jeans and our school shirts – our school shirts!'

'*And* they wouldn't let us bring our Nintendos,' chipped in Eryk.

'Don't worry,' said Liz. 'We can go and get them. We'll pick up some clothes, too.' She was pretty sure Tilly had a spare key for Gryzna's flat. 'Let's get you upstairs and settled in first.' She picked up the holdall and headed for the stairs.

'Liz?'

'What?' Liz turned.

Lukasz's face and voice were serious. 'We're happy to be here.'

Liz swallowed the lump that rose suddenly to her throat. 'And I'm glad to have you here,' she said when it had gone.

'What's for dinner? We're starved.'

THE HOTDOGS WENT DOWN WELL, but not quite as well as the donuts, which the boys devoured in a matter of seconds. When they'd finished, Liz made sure they washed their hands, and told them to put on their coats.

'Can we bring Nelson with us?' asked Lukasz.

'I don't see why not.'

'Sick!' said Eryk. 'I want to hold his lead.'

'It was me who asked. I'm going to hold it.'

'You can take turns,' said Liz, keen to avoid an argument so soon after their arrival. 'Five minutes each.'

'Me first!'

'No, me!'

'We'll toss a coin.' Liz reached for the change she kept in a saucer on the windowsill. 'Heads or tails?'

'Heads,' said Lukasz.

It was tails, so Eryk was put in charge of Nelson until they reached the Full Moon.

The café wasn't particularly busy, which was just as well, as there was only Tilly on the counter. She looked tired, but grinned when she saw the boys.

'Double trouble! How are you both?'

'Can we have a milkshake?'

'Please?'

Liz's eyes met Tilly's amused blue ones over their heads. 'Not just now,' Liz said, 'but we can maybe stop on the way back.' She ignored the boys' groans. 'I'm here for Gryzna's key?'

'It's in the back.' Tilly turned to the boys. 'I think Mags has some fresh brownies back there, too, if you want one?'

'Yeah!'

'Yes, please!'

They'd just had donuts. Liz tried not to think about the effect so much sugar might have on their behaviour as they all disappeared through the beaded curtain.

Liz looked around the café and saw a surprising figure at one of the tables by the window. It was Skipper Masterson, with his bushy beard, doing a crossword in his newspaper. Liz couldn't quite believe her luck. She approached his table and held out her hand.

'Hello,' she said brightly. 'You're Mr Masterson, aren't you? I'm Liz McLuckie. I don't think we've met.'

He shook her hand, clearly wondering who on earth she was. Liz squashed her own embarrassment and sat opposite him.

'I've never seen you in here before, have I?' she said conversationally.

'I don't usually have time to sit and do nothing in the middle of the day.'

There was an awkward pause.

She nodded at the crossword. 'Tricky one today, is it?'

Masterson scratched his beard. 'Not too bad. There's just one clue I'm struggling with.'

'Can I help?'

He lifted an eyebrow, then shrugged and read the clue aloud. '*Setting*. Seven letters, begins with a *C*, third letter *N*.'

Liz thought for a moment. 'Context.'

His eyes widened as he checked it. 'That's it, I think. Thanks.' He wrote the answer with his ballpoint pen.

'I saw you give your eulogy at Doc's funeral.' Liz couldn't think of a more natural way to steer the conversation.

His face shuttered again. 'Oh?'

'Very moving.'

He frowned. 'You think so?'

Liz nodded. 'A terrible tragedy.' She could hear Tilly's and the boys' voices in the kitchen and realised she didn't have long. 'Do you mind if I ask you a question?'

'Depends what it is.'

'How far out were you that night? When Doc went overboard?'

There was a beat of surprise; then Masterson scowled. 'That's hard to say. No one knows when it happened.'

'Of course.' Liz pressed on. 'I understand that. But where were you at midnight?'

He just looked at her.

'Midnight. Can you remember?'

'North of Sheringham Shoal somewhere.'

'How far out is that?'

Masterson pushed his chair back and stood up. He towered over Liz. 'With respect, Mrs McLuckie, I have enough to deal with, with my boat being out of action and no money coming in, without a complete stranger asking nosy questions.'

He stomped out just as Tilly and the boys reappeared

through the curtain. The bell on the door tinkled violently as he slammed it.

'Wow.' Tilly saw Liz was sitting at his table. 'Did you have anything to do with that?'

'I'm afraid so.'

'What on earth did you say to make him so mad?'

That was a very good question.

9

'What are you watching?' Eryk's voice, two inches from her ear, made Liz jump.

'The RNLI webcam.'

He peered more closely at her laptop screen, which showed a panoramic view of Whitby harbour taken from the Lifeboat Station on the Fish Pier.

'Lame.'

'You think so? I think it's pretty dramatic. Look at those waves out past the piers. White horses. It's pretty rough out there.'

Eryk just looked at her as if she had a screw loose. She decided to change the subject. 'Have you found your swimming trunks yet? We definitely brought them back with us yesterday.'

'They're not in the bag.'

'Maybe Lukasz has picked them up with his?' Liz went to the bottom of the stairs and yelled up them, 'Lukasz! Do you have Eryk's trunks up there?'

No answer.

'Go up and see,' she urged Eryk.

Eryk clattered up the stairs, almost colliding with Niall coming down. The young Irishman was all ready to go, with his own swimming roll tucked under one arm.

'Thanks, Niall. I really do appreciate this.'

'Don't be daft. I have a study week this week, so I'd only be sitting around pretending to read. We'll have a grand time, won't we, boys?'

The boys thumped down the stairs behind him.

'Can Nelson come?' asked Lukasz.

'No. He needs a proper walk.'

'Aww.'

'Come on, you two.' Niall shepherded them towards the door. 'Out.'

'Have you got your trunks, Eryk?' asked Liz.

'They were on his bed all the time,' said Lukasz. 'The divvy.'

Lukasz whacked Eryk over the head with his towel.

'Pack that in, you two!' snapped Niall. 'Out!'

It felt strange when they'd gone. Supernaturally quiet. The boys had been with her less than twenty-four hours, but Liz was already exhausted.

She shut down her laptop, put on her coat and woollens, and clipped Nelson onto his lead. Rather than take him for his favourite walk up the abbey steps to the churchyard, she decided to save herself a bit of time by taking him to the little viewing spot at the end of Henrietta Street, where the street ended – abruptly – in the sea. The last cottages of the terrace had been swept into the water by a landslide from the cliff a few years before. It was probably only a matter of time before Kipper and Gull went the same way, but Liz didn't mind. She would be long gone by then. She watched the choppy waters beyond the east pier while Nelson nosed along the fence and emptied his bladder; then they retraced their steps, past Kipper and Gull again, heading down

Church Street to the market square, the heart of the old town.

The town hall presided over the square in compact, neoclassical grandeur, its open ground floor flanked by Tuscan columns. Usually, the undercroft was crammed with market stalls, but today it was empty, so Liz was able to slip through it quickly to the other side, where she cut down past the Abbey Wharf restaurant to the Fish Pier and the RNLI Lifeboat Station.

The big all-weather rescue boat was moored in its usual spot beside the pier, riding the swell, resplendent in its dark blue and orange livery, but the building beside it showed no signs of life. There didn't seem to be a knocker or a bell on the door, so she went in. There was a staircase leading up, its walls lined with very neatly arranged framed black-and-white photos of past coxswains and crew. Liz tied Nelson to the bannister at the bottom.

'I won't be long. Behave yourself.' She ignored his accusing look and went up the stairs. At the top, she found herself in a lounge area with a view of the harbour. There was a kitchen alcove in the corner, but that was deserted, too.

'Hello?' called Liz. 'Is anybody here?'

She jumped as the door beside the kitchen alcove opened, framing a young man with spectacles and a moustache.

'Sorry, I didn't see you come in. Can I help you?'

'I have a question, about tides.'

'Then you've come to the right place. Would you mind joining me in here, though? I can't leave the radio.'

He beckoned her through the door into the small office, one wall of which was dominated by an old-fashioned-looking stack of technology that she assumed was the radio.

'I'm Martin, by the way,' said the young man. 'Section leader.' They shook hands. Liz thought he looked quite young to be in charge, but then scolded herself for the thought. It was a terrible habit of older people, to underestimate the age and capabilities of younger ones.

'I'm Liz McLuckie.'

The radio suddenly crackled with static and voices saying something about wind speed. Martin frowned.

'Is everything okay?' she asked.

'We have two walkers stranded on the cliffs near the Nab. The crew's attending in the inshore boat, but the swell's too high to reach them. We think the coastguard's going to have to winch them in from the top of the cliff. We're standing by, for now.'

'I don't mind coming back?'

'It's fine, honestly. I'm the least important cog in the machine... You said you had a question about tides?'

'I do.'

There were several charts pinned on the wall of the office. They looked very complicated, with swirling lines intersected by straighter ones – currents and shipping lanes, presumably – as well as patches of blue, and places marked with red pins. She had no idea what any of it might mean.

'Can you show me where Sheringham Shoal is?' she asked.

Martin went to one of the bigger charts, showing a long stretch of coastline from the Tees estuary right down to Great Yarmouth. He tapped a spot on it.

'There. Off the Norfolk coast.'

'Norfolk?'

'It isn't as far as it sounds. Only about thirty miles, as the crow flies, from Grimsby.'

'If someone went overboard there, hypothetically, how likely is it that they'd wash up here?'

'Here?'

'In the harbour?'

He frowned. 'Hypothetically? We're not talking about Doc Holliday, are we?'

Liz nodded. 'I think that's where the *Stella Mae* was when he went overboard. Sheringham Shoal, or somewhere close to it.'

'Really?' Martin was astonished. 'Are you sure?'

'Pretty sure.' Or was she? That was where Skipper Masterson had said the ship had been at midnight. It was possible, of course, that Daniel had gone overboard much later than that, when the boat was on her way home. 'How close would the *Stella* have to be for him to wash in here?'

'A couple of miles or so. Inside five-mile ground, anyway.'

Liz knew it was unlikely the boat could have made that much headway from Sheringham Shoal before dawn, in heavy seas, with a flooded engine.

It was clear from his puzzled expression that Martin knew it too.

'What should we do?' asked Liz. 'Should we tell the police?'

'I suppose so. If the *Stella* really was at Sheringham Shoal, there's definitely something strange going on.' He shrugged apologetically. 'I'm afraid you'll have to do it, though. I'm tied up here for now.'

SHE WENT BACK down the stairs to retrieve a fed-up-looking Nelson, and then tried calling Kevin on her mobile. It went straight to answerphone. She sighed. She really didn't want to go to the police station, but it looked as if she had no choice. But first, she had to take Nelson home.

Gull Cottage was still quiet when they got back. Liz guessed that Niall and the boys wouldn't be back from swimming for another hour or so. Nelson would be fine until then.

She settled him in his basket with a treat and headed out again.

Whitby Police Station was an unattractive red-brick '70s building at Spring Hill, just south of the town centre. It only took Liz fifteen minutes to get there, but she hesitated outside. She'd spent more time there than was respectable lately, and had even been a guest in one of the cells just a couple of months before. She straightened her shoulders and marched in.

Luckily, Kevin was the first person she saw inside. He was talking to one of the people sitting on the chairs in the waiting room. He glanced up as she entered, and his eyes widened.

'Excuse me just one second, will you?' he said to the woman he'd been talking to. He joined Liz. 'What are you doing here?'

'I tried calling you, but...'

'Is there something wrong?'

'I have some information. About Daniel Holliday. I think it's quite important.'

Kevin scratched his head. 'Okay, but come outside to tell me. I don't want—'

'Mrs McLuckie!' They were interrupted by a faux-bright female voice. 'Fancy seeing you here. I thought you would have had enough of our hospitality lately.' The upper half of DI Fiona Flint was framed by the hatch into the office. 'What can we do for you?'

'So you don't think Holliday should have washed up on Tate Hill beach?' Flint stared at Liz.

'Not if the *Stella Mae* was at Sheringham Shoal at midnight, when Doc sent his text.'

'It was the Grimsby mast that pinged,' volunteered Kevin.

'So that makes sense.'

Flint grunted. 'That mast covers a huge area, north and south. It proves nothing.' She turned to Liz, her eyes bright and hard. 'Sheringham Shoal. You're sure that's what Masterson said?'

Liz nodded. 'The station leader at the lifeboat station showed me where it is. It's miles from Whitby. I don't see how they could have made it back so fast in the storm.'

'I suppose we should at least look into it,' said Kevin.

'Of course we'll look into it!' snapped Flint. 'We'll have another word with Masterson. And with Martin Brooker.' She stood up. 'Okay, McLuckie. You can go.'

Kevin and Liz watched her stomp out, open-mouthed.

'Well, that's a first,' said Kevin.

Liz had to agree with him. That was the only time, ever, that Liz had presented Flint with evidence she hadn't sneered at, or that she hadn't threatened Liz for daring to get involved.

'Is she ill, do you think?' asked Liz.

Kevin grinned. 'I think it's because she's already sure it's murder. She has someone in her sights.'

'Who?'

'Christian Petit.'

'The Frenchman with the theft conviction?'

Kevin nodded. 'He hasn't been on the crew that long. And he had a massive bust-up with Holliday a couple of days before he died. A proper brawl, in the White Horse Tavern. Petit gave him a black eye, apparently.'

'Do you know what it was about?'

'Not yet. Everyone's very tight-lipped about it. Daniel Holliday's very much a sore point with everyone in the town at the moment.'

Liz supposed that was only natural. The last thing anyone would want to do was blab his private business to the police.

Kevin frowned. 'If the *Stella Mae* really was that far out at midnight, like Masterson says, that means Doc must have gone overboard much earlier than anyone thought. Probably just after they came out of the harbour.'

'Which means that someone else sent the text to Catriona.'

'And then threw his phone overboard.'

'Exactly,' said Liz. 'The question is, who?'

10

The next morning Eryk and Lukasz were up unfeasibly early, playing the TV in the sitting room far too loud. Liz threw on her dressing gown and hurried downstairs. She didn't want them to wake Niall, who'd been working late the night before in the Duke of York.

'Turn that down, please. Better still, turn it off.'

'But it's David Attenborough!' protested Lukasz.

'Whales!'

'It's educational!'

'It's also far too early.' Liz took the remote off Eryk and turned the volume down. She could hear scratching in the kitchen downstairs. 'Who wants to take Nelson for a walk?'

'Can we take him to see Mum?' asked Lukasz, hopefully.

Liz's heart squeezed. 'Not today.'

'So when can we see her?'

'Soon.' At least, Liz hoped so. Their lawyer, Caroline Burlington, had discovered where Gryzna was being detained, and was currently trying to negotiate access for the boys. But everything was just so damn slow. Liz thought a distraction was in order.

'Go and put your clothes on. Last one in the kitchen stinks!'

The boys eyed each other, then dashed for the door, elbowing each other out of the way. Liz hurried after them to put her own clothes on. She didn't want to stink.

INEVITABLY, of course, she was the last one down again.

'You stink!' crowed Lukasz.

'Ha ha ha.'

'You two didn't get dressed properly.' Lukasz was still wearing his pyjama bottoms, although his top half seemed to be in order. Eryk looked okay at first glance, but then she saw his jumper was inside out, and he had no socks on. 'You can't go out like that. Go and sort yourselves out.'

LIZ WAS EXHAUSTED by the time she finally managed to get them outside. It was still early, so they had the abbey steps to themselves as they climbed up. The boys ran on ahead with Nelson, leaving her to climb and count the steps on her own. It was her habit to count them, although she didn't really need to because every tenth step was marked with a brass Roman numeral. She paused halfway up, as usual, to catch her breath on one of the wider coffin steps and look at the view. It never failed to lift her spirits, even on a gloomy day like today.

Eighteenth-century Whitby lay below her – a jumble of cottages with red-tiled roofs still dark from the rain. Opposite, about half a mile away, was the West Cliff, with its grand Edwardian buildings and whale-bone arch. A stretch of sullen water lay in between – the harbour – where the two trawlers and a collection of smaller boats were moored. Liz could see the crime scene tape still fluttering on the decks of the *Stella Mae*. Surely the police couldn't keep it impounded for much longer?

She let the boys and Nelson expend some energy in the graveyard while she did a slow loop around the church. When she called them back to her, their faces were rosy again, and Nelson's tongue was lolling.

Liz looked at her watch. 'Come on,' she said. 'Let's see if we can persuade Tilly to open early and give us some breakfast.'

'Yay!'

CHURCH STREET WAS STILL quiet when they got to the bottom of the steps, with only the baker's and newsagent's open. Even though the Full Moon Café wasn't officially open until ten, Liz knew that Tilly and Mags would already be there. She and the boys cut through the town hall undercroft to Sandgate and peered through the café window.

'There's a light on,' said Lukasz. 'I can see it.'

Tilly appeared through the beaded curtain with a tray of pastries. Liz tapped on the window, and both boys joined in enthusiastically. Tilly hurried to unlock the door.

'Keep your ruddy hair on. Don't break my window!'

'Can we have some breakfast?' asked Lukasz.

'Pancakes!'

'I don't know about pancakes, but I have bacon and eggs?'

'Yay!'

Liz was just about to follow them all in when she saw someone heading towards her from the other end of Sandgate – a figure in a tweed coat and old-fashioned cloche hat, carrying two supermarket carrier bags.

'With you in a minute,' she called to Tilly.

She waited until Dora reached her.

'Morning, Dora.'

The museum curator just nodded and kept going.

'Dora!'

'What?' She turned.

'Don't be rude. How are things with you? Have you had any return visits?'

Dora looked blank, then realised what Liz was talking about. 'The burglars, you mean? No, they haven't come back.'

'Did you find out if they'd taken anything at all, when you'd the chance to tidy up?'

'No, they hadn't.' Dora peered at her. 'You're keeping that key safe, I hope?'

Liz nodded.

'Good. If Amanda turns up, I'll send her to you.' Dora stomped on her way.

Liz went into the café.

'Since when have you been so cosy with Dora Spackle?' Tilly, who was filling a teapot at the counter, had been watching the exchange through the window.

'I wouldn't call it cosy, exactly. I'm just helping her with something.'

'Something to do with Mandy Salthouse?'

'Sorry?'

'You were asking about Mandy, at Benedict's last week. I never did get the chance to ask you why.'

'I wasn't really asking about her. Just "Amandas" in general.'

'Isn't your friend called Amanda?' Mags had appeared with two milkshakes for the boys. She saw Tilly's blank look. 'The one you sometimes see on your day off?'

'Oh, yes.' Tilly dismissed it with a shrug. 'But she doesn't live in Whitby. You were asking about Amandas in the town, weren't you?'

'Yes.'

Tilly took the milkshakes from Mags and carried them to the boys' table. 'Right,' she said, 'who wants beans with their breakfast?'

'Me!'

'Me!'

After she'd had a cup of tea and some cinnamon toast, Liz took the opportunity to leave the boys in Tilly's care to run some errands. She had to buy stamps, a padded envelope and some bread, and knew she'd do it twice as fast on her own.

The post office was open, but already busy, as it was pension day. Liz had to wait in a sizeable queue of old folk to get her stamps and envelope. It was her sister Julie's birthday in a couple of weeks' time, so Liz needed the padded envelope to send her gifts to Kowloon, her last known address. She had no idea whether it would actually reach her or not, so hadn't bought her anything expensive – just some woollen socks, a bar of her favourite chocolate and half a dozen sachets of Marmite.

After the post office, she headed to the baker on Church Street. There was a queue there, too. An elegant young woman with straight blonde hair and a toddler in a buggy seemed to be holding things up as she rummaged desperately in her bag.

'I am sorry. I have it here somewhere.' She continued to search her bag, getting more and more frantic. '*Ou est-il. Je sais que c'est ici. Putain d'enfer!*'

Then, to the consternation of everyone in the shop, she burst into tears.

'*Puis-je vous aider?*' On hearing the woman speak French, Liz had crept to the front.

The young woman's head snapped up, and she wiped her face. '*Ma carte bancaire. Je l'ai oublie.*'

'*Ne vous inquietez pas.*' Liz hoped her French wasn't too

terrible. '*Laissez moi vous aider.*' Then she spoke to the bewildered baker's assistant, whom she knew well. 'I'll pay for the lady's things, Flora.'

The young Frenchwoman looked on, pink-faced, as Flora processed her payment with Liz's card. 'I will pay you back,' she said to Liz. 'I am so embarrassed.'

'Please don't worry. You're Mrs Petit, aren't you?'

'Juliette. But how did you know?'

'There can't be many Frenchwomen in Whitby.'

'Ah, no, there aren't. *Malheureusement.*' She packed her shopping in the net under the buggy. The toddler in it was fast asleep and snoring. They made their way back out through the shop, and Liz helped lift the buggy down the steps.

'I must pay you back,' said Juliette Petit.

'There's no hurry. I'll give you my number.'

'No, no! You must come home with me now. It is not far... Unless, of course, you are too busy?'

Liz thought about it. She knew Lukasz and Eryk would be okay at the café, and she was curious about this elegant, forgetful Frenchwoman.

As Juliette had promised, she didn't live far, in one of the blocks of flats on the East Quay, at the far end of Church Street. Built sometime in the thirties or forties, they were accessed by staircases and balconies at the back.

'How on earth do you manage the buggy on your own up all these steps?'

'Pfffft!' Juliette shrugged. 'I am stronger than I look.' She opened the door with her key. 'You must excuse the state of the flat. I was not expecting a visitor.'

The flat was actually quite tidy, although, from the lack of carpets and the sparse furnishings, it was clear the Petits didn't have a lot of money. Juliette parked the buggy in the corner to let the still-sleeping toddler carry on snoozing. 'She was up at three this morning,' she explained. 'The teeth, you know.'

'Teething.'

'*Exactement*. Please, sit yourself. Would you like some coffee?'

'Coffee would be lovely.' Liz didn't usually drink coffee, but didn't want to inconvenience Juliette by asking for tea. She guessed that, as a Frenchwoman, she would be a committed coffee drinker. Her suspicion was proved right when Juliette carefully measured coffee grounds into a stovetop cafetiere.

'You like it strong?'

'Not too strong, please.'

Juliette nodded.

'Is your husband here?' asked Liz.

'*Non*. He is away, in Grimsby. Looking for work.'

'But I thought... isn't he on the *Stella Mae* crew?'

'He was. But now' – Juliette shrugged – 'now he has been told there will be no place for him when the boat is released.'

The hiss of the cafetiere on the stove filled an awkward silence. Juliette gazed at Liz, as if assessing her. 'The thing is,' she said, 'he was not entirely honest when he joined the crew. He has, how you say, something of a troubled past?'

His police record. 'I see. And Skipper Masterson found out when the police started their investigation?'

'*Precisement*.' Juliette poured them both a mug of coffee. 'Cream?'

'Yes, please.'

She added a generous splash of cream to Liz's mug and handed it to her. 'The pity of it is that Christian is now going direct.'

Liz guessed she meant *straight*.

'And I am just starting to feel at home.' Juliette gestured to the bare kitchen. 'I know it does not look like much, but it is a beginning, *non*?'

Liz nodded.

Juliette continued, 'You would think Skipper Masterson would overlook Christian's *"petit mensonge"*. He will be short-handed by one crew member already, will he not, when the *Stella Mae* sails again?'

That was true, if a little callous to point out. French pragmatism in action.

Juliette shrugged. 'If I am honest, I think the skipper is using the situation as an excuse. Christian did not get on so well with the rest of his crew. They held him... how do you say?... at the end of their arms?'

'At arm's length.' Liz nodded. 'I heard he'd had a fight. With Daniel Holliday.'

'A fight?' Juliette's eyebrows disappeared under her fringe.

Liz realised she'd been indiscreet, and hurried to take it back. 'But maybe I got that wrong.'

'It would not surprise me.' Juliette shook her head sadly. 'Do you know, you are the very first person to talk to me, properly, in two months? The fact is that we are outsiders in Whitby and always will be.'

Liz leapt to defend Whitby's honour. 'I haven't found that. I moved here from Scotland, and everyone was very welcoming.'

'Yes, but you are British, *non*?'

'Even so. I have friends who aren't who've settled in well here.' Then Liz remembered poor Gryzna sitting in a detention centre somewhere. But that was the system that was at fault, not the people. 'You know, I've generally found that you get out what you put in.'

'*Pardon?*'

'You have to make an effort to make friends.' She guessed

that Juliette might find that tricky. 'It can be hard, but it is worth it.'

'Perhaps you are right.' Juliette nodded glumly. 'Perhaps I have not been so willing. But it hardly seems worth it now, does it?'

'It's never too late,' said Liz. 'And look, here I am. You have one friend.'

'That I owe money to. Please remind me how much?'

Really? Liz tried to disguise her dismay. Perhaps it wasn't so very surprising Juliette had difficulty making friends.

They both started as they heard a key in the lock. Christian Petit let himself in. He was a tall man with pleasant features and a careworn expression.

Juliette hurried to hug him. '*Tu rentres tot, non?*'

'*Je n'ai pas eu de chance. Tous les chalutiers sont remplis.*' He spotted Liz and gave Juliette a puzzled look.

'This is Mrs McLuckie.' Juliette hurried to introduce them. 'She has been a great help to me today.'

'Pleased to meet you, Mrs McLuckie.'

'Liz.'

'Liz.' Christian smiled. It lit up his whole face, turning what had seemed merely pleasant into very attractive indeed. Liz could see what had drawn his glamorous wife to him.

A thin cry cut through the air. The baby stretched out her little feet and scrunched up her face. Christian lifted her tenderly out of her buggy and put her on his shoulder.

'*Doucement, ma cherie. Ton papa est la.*'

Liz realised she was intruding, finished her coffee quickly and made her excuses to leave.

As she negotiated the balconies and staircases at the back of the flat, Liz came to a conclusion. Christian Petit might have got into an altercation with Daniel before he died, but – call her naïve – he really didn't seem like a killer.

· · ·

SHE WAS RETRACING her steps to the baker's to buy the bread she hadn't bought the first time, when her mobile rang. It was Benedict.

'Hi. What kind of day are you having?'

'Quite interesting.'

'Are the boys behaving themselves?'

'So far. They're at the café just now while I run some errands.'

'I was wondering whether I should bring my toothbrush when I come for dinner tonight.'

Liz hesitated. 'I don't know. I want the boys to feel settled before I introduce any new elements.'

'New elements? It's not as if they don't know me, Liz.'

'I know... I know... it's just they don't know we're together, do they? And I don't know how I feel about us being... together... with them in the same house.'

There was a long pause. When Benedict did speak, he sounded crestfallen. 'That isn't likely to change any time soon, is it?'

That was true. Caroline Burlington still hadn't been able to give them any idea of the timeline involved in Gryzna's appeal.

'Let's just give things a few days to settle down, B.'

'Okay. Of course.' He sounded brighter, but Liz guessed he'd had to make an effort. 'I'll bring some wine, shall I? Red or white?'

'I don't know. What goes with hotdogs and chips?'

IT WASN'T until much later that night, after they'd all had dinner, and Benedict had gone home again, that Liz had any headspace for Juliette Petit. She thought about her as she put her pyjamas on. It was clear she had no idea Christian and

Daniel had even come to blows, much less what it might have been about.

Liz turned off her bedside light and lay in the dark for a few minutes before realising she was wide awake and wasn't likely to go to sleep any time soon. She sat up, turned her light on again, and felt underneath the mattress for Daniel Holliday's key. It was a very ordinary key. Most probably for an old padlock, but which padlock, where? She returned the key to its hiding place and switched the light off again.

But still her mind churned. Who was the mysterious Amanda? Was she the veiled woman who had been at Daniel's funeral? Who had broken into Dora's cottage – was it the key they were after? It seemed likely, as they hadn't taken anything else. Why had Daniel told Dora not to give the key to the police? Had he thought someone might be after him? Why would someone be after him? Could it be Christian Petit? What had their fight in the White Horse been about? When exactly had Daniel gone overboard from the *Stella Mae*? Who had sent the text to Catriona? Christian Petit? Billy Howson?

Was Billy having an affair with Catriona? Liz really hoped not. She couldn't imagine how Mike and Lesley would take it if they found out – or, worse, discovered their son was a murderer. But if Billy *did* have something to do with Daniel's death, who was Amanda, and where did she fit in?

Realising she was going round in circles, she made an effort to stop thinking about Daniel Holliday. She thought about Benedict instead. Their relationship had taken a distinct nose-dive since the boys had arrived. Examining her feelings about that, Liz realised she was disappointed and frustrated with herself, and that those emotions were also mixed with something else... a teeny bit of relief? Had their relationship been moving too fast?

She eventually fell asleep in the early hours of the morning.

She woke with a jump just moments later as thunder crashed overhead. A flash of bright white light ripped through the room. Liz sat up, electrified. She'd remembered something! Something Skipper Masterson had said in his eulogy at the funeral. It might not mean anything, but on the other hand, it might just be the clue that could lead her to Daniel Holliday's missing padlock.

11

'Do you know if there are any allotments in the town?' Liz managed to catch Mike Howson making his morning delivery to the smokehouse. Born and bred in Whitby, he knew everything and everyone.

'Taking up gardening, are you, Mrs Mac?'

'Maybe.' In his eulogy at the funeral, Skipper Masterson had mentioned that Daniel Holliday enjoyed gardening, yet the flat he shared with Catriona on New Quay Road was in a modern block. Gardenless. So where did he garden?

'Well, now, let me think.' Mike scratched his head. 'There's three, far as I can remember – Stakesby Vale, Cholmley, and California Beck. I imagine there's waiting lists for all three of them. If you're keen, you should get your name down sooner rather than later.'

Liz nodded. 'Will do.'

He nodded and went on his way.

'Mike!' she called him back. 'I don't suppose you know any Amandas in the town, do you?'

'Amanda? Well, there was old Mandy Salthouse, but she passed away last year, God rest her. Apart from that, the only

Amanda I can think of is Amanda Younger, Neil Younger's girl, up on St Peter's Road.'

'How old is she?'

'About twelve.'

'Oh.' Definitely not the Amanda she was looking for. 'Thanks.'

Liz went back inside. If Daniel Holliday had an allotment, the council would probably have his name on a register of some kind, which could tell her where his plot was. Most allotments had sheds. And most sheds, padlocks.

Nelson whined and lifted his nose into the air.

Liz sniffed. There was an odd smell. Burning? Her heart plummeted. Not another fire! She hurried up the stairs to find the source of the smell before the fire alarms went off. It was definitely stronger on the landing. It seemed to be coming from the boys' room. She knocked at the door and went in.

The room was full of candles. Lit candles. The boys were sitting on the floor, dressed only in their pyjama bottoms.

'What are you doing?' gasped Liz.

'A spell. To get Mum back,' explained Lukasz. 'You're spoiling it.'

But Liz was already in motion, blowing out the candles closest to her. 'Put them out! Candles are dangerous.'

'You're breaking our spell!'

'I don't care! Open flames are dangerous.' She couldn't risk another fire like the one that had damaged the cottage the previous October. It had taken her months to repair the damage. 'Blow them out! Now!'

It took them a while to get round them all, but eventually all the candles were extinguished. She opened the window.

'What did you do that for?' Lukasz sulked. 'It was working.'

'I doubt it.' She picked up a book from the floor – *Common Magik.* 'Where on earth did you get this?'

'From the café. We borrowed it.'

'Did Tilly lend it to you?' Tilly and Mags had a reading area in the café and also sold a small selection of New Age books.

'No. We *borrowed* it.'

'You can't just take things without asking. That's not borrowing, it's stealing.'

'Not if you take it back,' protested Lukasz.

'We were going to take it back,' said Eryk.

'Get some clothes on. I'm going to ring the council. It's about time you two were back at school.'

'No!' Lukasz stamped his foot. 'We don't want to go back. We're too busy. We don't have time.'

'If you have time for "*magik*", you have time for school. Clothes on, now.'

The council had taken the boys out of West Cliff Primary School to move them to Middlesbrough, but it was clearly time they were reinstated. They needed the mental stimulation. Liz thought that a visit to the council in person might be more effective than a phone call.

She went downstairs and patted Nelson to reassure him.

'What's all the racket about?' Niall appeared at the bottom of the stairs, rubbing his eyes.

'Nothing. Or not much. Sorry we woke you.'

'It's fine. I had to get up anyway. I have classes at eleven.'

Liz squashed her disappointment. She'd been counting on him to babysit the boys while she paid a visit to the council. When Niall went back upstairs to shower, she called Tilly.

'I don't suppose you could take the boys again for an hour or two?'

'Oh, Liz, you know I would, but we have a funeral party

coming in at eleven. The boys and a group of grieving relatives really wouldn't mix.'

'Ah. Okay. Don't worry, I'll think of something else.' Benedict, Kevin and Irwin would all be working. 'I'll call Iris. See if she's busy.'

'You haven't forgotten about our meeting at lunchtime?'

Caroline Burlington was coming to Benedict's to discuss Gryzna's case. Everyone had promised to be there if they could.

'No, I'll be there.' Liz was about to hang up when she remembered something. 'Oh, by the way, I think you're missing a book.'

LUCKILY, Iris and Dickie were up for a visit from the boys. Liz dropped Eryk and Lukasz at the Anchorage Retirement Home, with a stern warning to behave themselves, then headed to the council headquarters.

Pannet Park was a public space, a green jewel in the middle of the town, threaded with winding pathways and dotted with interesting plants. At the centre of the park sat the Pannet Art Gallery and Museum, a classical red-brick building with an impressive white portico and columns. The original building was still intact, with the addition of a modern grey roof that could have distracted from the historical charm of the building, but actually managed to enhance it. It housed an eclectic collection of art and artifacts, and – rather unexpectedly – the council offices.

It took Liz almost an hour with the social worker, but when she was done, the boys were scheduled to return to West Cliff Primary the following Monday. Liz felt guilty in one way – the boys had had a rough time of it lately – but on the other hand, she knew it was better for them in the long run. Better for them and her own sanity.

As she was coming out, a thought occurred to her – she could kill two birds with one stone. She stopped at reception.

'Is it possible to talk to someone in the parks and recreation department?'

'About what exactly?'

'Allotments.'

'Hold on a moment. I'll get someone for you.'

While she waited, Liz formulated a plan to get the information she needed.

'Yes?' A man of about thirty replaced the receptionist at the desk. He had thick spectacles and was dressed unexpectedly casually in a Metallica tee shirt. Liz imagined he didn't usually talk to members of the public face-to-face.

'I'd like to talk to you about one of your allotment holders. Daniel Holliday.'

'He's dead.'

'I know.' Liz eyed him. As she'd suspected, he clearly wasn't used to dealing with people. 'The thing is, I lent him my gardening shears.'

He blinked at her through his thick lenses. 'It's up to his family to clear the plot of his personal belongings before we let it out again. They haven't been in touch with us yet.'

'I really don't want to bother Catriona about something so trivial.'

His expression clearly said, *so why bother me with it?*

'My shears have sentimental value.'

'Gardening shears?'

She ignored his tone of disbelief. 'They were my husband's. His favourite pair.' She pressed on. 'I was wondering if you could tell me exactly where Daniel's allotment is. I could just go and have a look around. He might have left them lying about somewhere. Then I wouldn't have to bother Catriona.'

The clerk just looked at her.

'Poor Catriona,' said Liz. 'She's had so much to deal with already.'

The clerk rolled his eyes, actually rolled his eyes, but did what Liz was hoping he would do – he turned to the computer on the desk and tapped a few keys.

'Mr Daniel Holliday. Has plot number twelve on Cholmley allotments.'

'Number twelve? Are the allotments clearly numbered?'

'Not as a rule, no.'

'So...?'

The clerk sighed and swivelled the computer screen around so Liz could see the map of the allotments.

'Right there.' He tapped a spot on the map. 'Plot twelve.'

Cholmley was on the East Cliff, beside the abbey. More precisely, it was beside the youth hostel, beside the abbey. Plot twelve was on the other side of the boundary wall of the main block of allotments and, rather perversely, the tenth plot in from the footpath. She beamed at the clerk. 'Thank you so much.'

WITH THE TWINS safely in Iris's charge – she hoped – Liz realised there was no time like the present to take a look at Daniel's allotment. She didn't have the key with her, but thought it couldn't hurt to scout things out and see if there was a shed.

It was quite a hike to get there from Pannet Park. She had to head back through the town, over the swing bridge to the old town, all the way up the abbey steps, and then take the path at the top of the cliff that skirted the medieval outbuildings of the museum and youth hostel. The path traced the edge of the Donkey Field, which was where the beach ride donkeys used to be kept in the days when animal welfare wasn't so high a priority. The field was still home to a couple of well-fed ponies, but they were no longer used for hard labour.

At the end of the run of medieval buildings, Liz found a gate in the wall, with a sign that said PRIVATE. It had a square hole in it. When she stood on tiptoe to peer through, she could see rows of well-kept allotments inside. She didn't think that was what she was looking for. From the map she'd seen, plot twelve lay outside the medieval wall. She continued on to where the wall stopped and the main path dropped steeply down the hill towards the east quay. The wall hadn't actually stopped, of course, but had only turned the corner to the left, where there was a collection of much smaller, more ramshackle plots – less like allotments, and more like a shanty town growing in the shade of the old medieval wall. Liz took the path that ran beside them, pleased to see that most had storage sheds or pigeon lofts, although some were very makeshift, cobbled together from recycled material. She counted the plots as she passed until she came to the tenth one in from the path. It was bounded by a rickety wooden fence and overgrown with weeds and brambles – hardly evidence of a keen gardener. At the back, beside the wall, there was a small shed. Liz pushed her way in through the rotten gate to take a closer look. The shed had a window, but it was blocked with cardboard inside, so she couldn't see in. The door was secured with an old padlock. The rust on the padlock was exactly the same shade as the rust on the key under her mattress.

Liz was aching to tell Dora about her discovery, and to get the key to see if it fit, but knew she was going to have to curb her impatience for now. She had to get back down the hill, pronto, and over to the West Cliff to pick up the boys from the Anchorage, if she was to have any hope of making the meeting with Caroline Burlington at one o'clock.

'I DIDN'T THINK YOU WERE COMING,' bellowed Iris

when she saw Liz appear in the residents' lounge. The boys were playing cards with Dickie and another couple of Anchorage residents Liz didn't know. By the heap of copper coins at Eryk's elbow, they'd either been at it some time, or he was fleecing them royally.

'Look, Liz,' said Eryk when he spotted her. 'I've won hundreds!'

'He doesn't even cheat,' said Lukasz, impressed.

Liz wasn't sure about the ethics of playing cards for money with kids, but she didn't have time to debate it with Iris or her friends. She thought they'd probably learned their lesson anyway. 'Come on, collect your winnings. We need to get on.'

'ME AND DICKIE ARE COMING WITH YOU.'

'What's that?' asked Dickie.

'I SAID WE'RE GOING WITH THEM. WE WANT TO HEAR WHAT THAT HOTSHOT LAWYER HAS TO SAY FOR HERSELF.'

Dickie nodded. 'We do.'

'What's a lawyer?' asked Lukasz.

'I'll tell you on the way. Come on, let's go, or we'll be late.'

THEY ARRIVED at Benedict's house at exactly the same time as Caroline Burlington parked her Mercedes roadster by the gate. Lukasz gave a low whistle.

'Is that the lawyer?' he asked.

Liz nodded.

'I'm definitely going to be a lawyer when I grow up.'

'I'm not,' said Eryk. 'I'm going to be a poker player.'

They all watched as Caroline got out of her car and approached them. She was very well put-together, with shiny, expensively coloured hair and an immaculate skirt suit. Liz couldn't imagine she would make much money only doing immigration work, so deduced that she took on other kinds of cases too.

'I'M IRIS GLADWELL. THIS IS MY FRIEND DICKIE LEDGARD. PLEASED TO MEET YOU.' Iris practically curtseyed as she pumped Caroline's hand. To Caroline's credit, she looked only slightly alarmed.

The door behind them opened.

'I thought I heard voices out here,' said Benedict. 'Come on in, or you'll freeze.'

After persuading the boys to go upstairs to watch TV, and bribing them with hot chocolate to stay put, everyone sat around the large kitchen table. Irwin, Kevin and Tilly were there, but not Mags, who'd had to stay in the café.

'The good news is that I managed to lodge our appeal before the deadline,' said Caroline when everyone had been introduced. 'I've detailed all the facts of the case to the Home Office, including that Mr Polonsky "disappeared" while in detention in Belarus.'

Everyone exchanged horrified looks. Only Liz had known about that.

Caroline continued, 'I am hopeful the appeal will be successful, but it might be some time before we hear.'

'They won't deport her in the meantime?' asked Benedict.

'Not before the appeal is heard.'

'That's something, at least,' said Tilly.

'Is it possible to visit her?' asked Liz. 'Where is she?'

'The detention centre in Middlesbrough. I'm afraid there are a lot of hoops to jump through, and a lot of red tape for visits. You might be better off sitting tight for now and not rocking the boat.'

Liz heard a muffled noise at the door into the hallway. It was slightly ajar. Maybe hot chocolate wasn't such an effective bribe after all.

'What did she say?' asked Dickie. 'I missed that last bit.'

'SHE SAID WE SHOULDN'T ROCK THE BOAT.'

'What boat?'

'What about the boys?' asked Kevin, ignoring him. 'What will happen to them if they do deport her?'

'Let's not worry about that for now. I suggest we all keep our hopes up.' Caroline looked around at them all. 'I really have to say that Mrs Polonsky is a lucky woman, to have such very good friends.'

12

'That can't be it,' said Dora, eyeing the shed from the allotment gate.

'What were you expecting?'

Dora pulled a face. 'It hardly looks like he'd keep anything valuable in there.'

She had a point, but Liz shrugged. 'We don't even know if the key fits yet, do we?'

She climbed over the rotten gate. Dora glanced nervously around. It was too early for there to be many people about – the sun was barely up and hadn't even started to thaw the frost on the long grass and brambles. A slight mist rose from the frozen ground, giving the run-down jumble of allotments an eerie air.

'Careful, that wood's quite splintery.' Liz averted her eyes from a flash of matronly gusset as Dora climbed over the gate.

'I can manage, thank you very much.' Dora straightened her skirt and joined her next to the shed. 'Where's the key?'

Liz took it out and drew a deep breath. The moment of truth.

'Get on with it,' snapped Dora. 'Don't make a meal of it.'

Liz resisted the urge to strangle her with her tweed scarf, and put the key into the lock instead.

It turned easily, and the padlock snapped open.

'The slipper fits!'

Dora pushed the door open. 'It's pitch black in there. I can't see a thing.'

'Luckily,' said Liz, whipping her torch from her pocket like a gunslinger, 'I came prepared.' She shone the beam around the inside of the shed, ignoring the symphony of scuttlings and scratchings that accompanied it. It revealed that the shed was empty apart from an old exercise bike draped in cobwebs, and a filing cabinet.

Liz went to the filing cabinet. It was locked.

'Damn.'

'Let's smash it open with something.'

'We can't do that,' said Liz, horrified.

'Why not? It's just an old filing cabinet. Look, here's something we can use.' Dora picked a dirty screwdriver off the floor.

Liz hesitated. Technically, the filing cabinet and everything in it belonged to Catriona, but Daniel *had* left the padlock key in Dora's care. And, if Liz was honest, she was itching to see what was inside.

Dora was watching her, her face illuminated in the torchlight. 'Well?'

'Okay. Give me that.'

The top drawer of the filing cabinet didn't put up much of a fight. After only a couple of seconds of being attacked by the screwdriver, it surrendered with a crack.

'What's inside? Let me see.' Dora elbowed Liz out of the way and pulled a thick paper file from the top drawer. Liz checked the other drawers: all empty.

Dora pulled a face. 'Not much, is it?'

'Let's take it somewhere to look at it properly,' said Liz. 'I'm freezing.'

They were just about to move towards the door when they heard a noise outside – there was someone coming along the path. Dora's eyes opened wide. Liz quickly switched the torch off. They waited for whoever it was to pass, but, to their horror, they stopped at the allotment right next door.

'Come on, my lovelies,' said a male voice. 'Breakfast time.'

They heard him unlocking the pigeon loft.

'What are we going to do?' breathed Dora.

'We'll just have to wait until he's gone,' whispered Liz.

Liz poked a hole in the cardboard at the window and peeked out. She could see a man in a bright red jacket busying himself at the pigeon loft next door. There was no way they could leave without him seeing them.

They waited for what seemed like a lifetime while the man greeted each and every one of his birds individually and at length before feeding them. By the time he had eventually finished and was locking the loft again, Liz thought she would never be warm again. They waited until his footsteps had gone before they crept out.

'That was dreadful,' said Dora. 'I thought I was going to be trapped in there forever with you. I can't imagine anything worse.'

THEY TOOK the file to Dora's cottage and warmed up with a pot of tea before opening the file at the kitchen table.

'Look, there's a passport in here,' said Dora. She opened it and frowned.

'What?' asked Liz. Dora gave her the passport. It had a photo of Daniel, but the name on it wasn't Daniel Holliday, it was Daniel Poulson.

'How odd,' said Liz. 'He wasn't adopted or anything, was he?'

Dora shook her head. 'Definitely not.' She pulled some more papers out of the file – a car ownership registration, MOT papers and a car insurance policy, all in the name of Daniel Poulson. There was also a tenancy agreement – 63 Lower Darnborough Street, York – again, in the name of Daniel Poulson.

'We should take these to the police,' said Liz.

'Absolutely not! It's none of their business.'

'But, Dora, this doesn't look good. Who knows what Daniel was involved in?'

'All the more reason to keep it in the family.' Dora saw Liz's doubtful expression. 'At least let's try to get to the bottom of this. If it turns out Daniel was doing anything illegal, then we'll go to the police.'

'I'm not sure how legal it is to have two different names.'

'Come with me to York.' Dora waved the tenancy agreement. 'Let's see what's going on.'

Liz sighed. 'If he was involved in anything, it's possible his death had something to do with it. We could be putting ourselves in danger.'

'Danger!' Dora gave a derisive snort. 'Who's going to bother about two middle-aged ladies?'

Liz wasn't sure she was convinced by Dora's bravado. Dora had been quite freaked out by her burglary.

'Please.' Dora's eyes implored her through her spectacles.

Liz sighed. 'Okay. I suppose we can go on Monday. The twins will be back at school then.'

'Good. I don't have a car. You can drive us.'

THE NEXT DAY was changeover day. After saying goodbye to the Yarrows, Liz prepared Kipper for her next tenants. The boys gave her a hand, stripping the bed while she cleared out the rubbish and cleaned the fridge. It took her about half an hour. It wasn't until she was finished that she realised the boys had gone very quiet upstairs.

'Eryk! Lukasz! Do you have those sheets?'

No reply. Liz took the clean linen from her bag and took it upstairs. She found the boys had made a make-shift den with the dirty sheets, draping a sheet from the bottom of the bed to the chest of drawers under the window.

'Is this a private party, or can anyone join in?' She stuck her head into the den. 'Are you two having fun?'

'Not really, no,' said Lukasz. They looked at her solemnly. Both had been very quiet ever since Caroline's visit to Benedict's. Liz wondered whether they *had* been listening at the door.

'Okay.' Liz was at a bit of a loss for what to say. 'Well, let's get these dirty sheets into the laundry bag and get the new ones on.'

'Why do we have to help you?' asked Lukasz.

'We're not servants,' added Eryk.

'You don't have to help if you don't want to. I thought you might enjoy it, that's all.'

'We don't.'

'Okay, sit over there while I finish with the bed.'

Liz made up the bed in silence, watched by the twins. Then she double-checked everything was ready for the new tenant, locked the door and put the key in the key safe.

'Are we going home now?' asked Eryk.

'Home?' Lukasz glared at him.

Eryk corrected himself. 'Are we going back to your cottage now?'

'No, we have to take the dirty sheets to the launderette.' Her own washing machine was too old and too temperamental to trust with the letting linen.

'Do we have to come?'

'Yes. No arguments, please.' Niall was working, and she had no intention of leaving the boys on their own in Gull Cottage for any length of time, no matter how hard they pleaded.

'Then can we bring Nelson?'

'If you like.'

They popped into Gull to collect Nelson, then set off for the West Cliff. The weather was still squally. No one was hanging around on the streets, but only doing whatever it was they had to do before hurrying straight home again. Seagulls wheeled and yodelled overhead.

'Can we go in the amusements?' asked Lukasz as they passed the arcades on the quayside. Even though there was no one around, the lights were flashing enticingly.

'Maybe later. Let's get this lot up to the launderette first.'

They climbed the steps up the Khyber Pass, to the whalebone arch. As they reached the top of the steps, she spotted a figure on one of the bench seats, hunched over against the wind.

'Potsy, what are you doing out here?'

'Nothing much.' He blinked at her through rain-splashed spectacles as he petted Nelson. 'Mum says I have to get some fresh air. Where are you going? Somewhere nice?'

Liz realised he must have very little to do, and even less money to do it with, now the *Stella Mae* was out of action. She had an idea.

'Could you do me a massive favour? Could you please take the boys down to the amusements? Just for half an hour? It would be such a help.'

The boys grinned at each other.

Potsy puffed himself up. 'You know me, Mrs Mac, always pleased to help if I can.'

Liz gave him some money from her purse. 'Get yourselves

a hot drink, too. Not coffee for the boys – no caffeine. Hot chocolate.'

'Hot chocolate, yay!'

'Can we take Nelson too?'

'I don't think they let dogs in the arcades. I'll keep him with me.'

She waved them off and watched as they headed eagerly back down the steps to the quayside. She hoped she'd done the right thing. She felt fairly confident she could trust Potsy with the boys, at least for a little while.

She hurried to the launderette on the esplanade, where she swapped her dirty bedsheets for the clean ones she'd dropped off the week before, then headed back down to the quayside. Crime scene tape was still fluttering on the *Stella Mae*, but there was no police presence there. Liz thought that was maybe a good sign that the forensics had been completed. She found Potsy and the boys in PennyCity, one of the more garish arcades, which was owned by Phil Nethergate, a local 'businessman' she'd fallen foul of the summer before.

'Can we have some more money?' asked Lukasz. 'I have none left.'

'Me neither,' said Eryk.

'You've spent it already?' She looked at Potsy for confirmation, but he just shrugged. 'It's time to go home anyway,' said Liz.

Potsy looked crestfallen.

'Why don't you come and have some lunch with us?'

He beamed. 'If it's not too much trouble, Mrs Mac.'

LIZ MADE everyone sausage and beans for lunch when they got back to Gull Cottage. She pretended not to see Potsy slipping Nelson one of his sausages under the table.

'Do you know when they're going to release the *Stella Mae*?' she asked him.

'Soon, Skipper reckons. Leastways, he hopes so. He needs the money, you know.'

'Does he?'

Potsy nodded. 'He had the boat refurnished in the summer.'

Liz assumed he meant refurbished.

'It cost him a lot of money. He had to borrow it.' Potsy had no idea he was being indiscreet.

'Who did he borrow it from? The bank?' Liz felt a little guilty to be taking advantage.

'No. Phil Nethergate.'

'I thought he was in prison.'

'Oh, he is. But Mrs Nethergate runs things now. She wants her money back, Skipper says.'

Liz didn't envy being in Masterson's shoes, owing the Nethergates money. If Phil's wife was anything like her husband, she wouldn't pull punches when it came to getting her money back.

'Doc owed Mrs Nethergate money, too.' Potsy chewed happily on his sausage and took a huge swig of tea.

Liz's ears pricked up. 'Did he?' If Daniel was involved with the Nethergates, that made it even more likely that he was up to no good with his fake identity.

'A LOT of money, Billy says.'

Liz stared at him. How had Daniel managed to run up a big debt? Did he have a gambling problem? A drug addiction? Could the Nethergates have killed Daniel to make an example of him? Liz knew that Phil was capable of blackmail, intimidation, and actual bodily harm when it suited him... but murder? They had to have somehow gained access to the *Stella Mae*, which meant they had to have an accomplice on the boat.

Someone they had leverage over. Someone like Skipper Masterson?

'Billy says the sooner we get back on the boat and start earning the skipper money again, the better.' Potsy's brow crinkled with concern. 'Or we could lose our jobs.'

'I'm sure it won't come to that.' She wanted to reassure him, but he stared glumly into his mug. She thought a change of subject might help.

'You drink at the White Horse, Potsy, don't you?'

'I do. Me and the lads.'

'Christian Petit too?'

Potsy frowned. 'No, I like Chris, but he doesn't drink with us. Not anymore. Not since...' He tailed off, unsure whether he should continue.

'Not since he had that fight with Daniel?'

'Yes.' Potsy looked relieved that Liz already knew about it. 'Not since then. He gave Daniel a proper black eye.'

'Do you know why?'

Potsy gave her a puzzled look.

'Do you know what the fight was about?'

'Doc said something not very nice about Chris's wife. Mrs Petit. The lads reckon Doc deserved it. He wasn't very nice about women sometimes. I wish Chris would come to the White Horse with us again.'

Liz wondered whether Potsy knew that Christian had been fired from the crew, and decided not to mention it. It might upset him.

'Do we have any ice cream?' asked Lukasz, who had hoovered up his beans and was now licking his plate.

'In the freezer. Isn't it a bit cold for ice cream, though?'

The boys and Potsy looked at her as if she were mad.

'It's never too cold for ice cream, Mrs Mac,' said Potsy. 'Everyone knows that.'

Liz watched the three of them as they squabbled over the

ice cream. Potsy had inadvertently told her a lot of things she hadn't known – that the fight in the White Horse had been about Juliette Petit, or at least about some misogynistic comment Daniel had made about her, and that both Daniel and Skipper Masterson owed the Nethergates money.

But did any of it have anything to do with Daniel's death?

13

'Did you know that Daniel Holliday owed the Nethergates money?'

Kevin looked thoughtful. 'No. But that's very interesting. Hermione Nethergate has taken over her husband's business. The part of it we didn't shut down, anyway. Looks like it hasn't taken her long to resurrect the loan sharking.'

Liz had been avoiding Kevin because she was feeling guilty about not telling him about the paperwork she and Dora had found at the allotment. She reckoned the information about the Nethergates was a safe enough thing to tell him. He'd volunteered to take the twins to school, and, to their delight, had turned up in a squad car.

'Come on, you two, hurry up!' he called up the stairs. 'I'm blocking the street.'

The boys thumped down the stairs.

'Can we put the lights on?'

'And the siren?'

Kevin winked at Liz. 'We'll see; get your coats on.'

'Do you have your packed lunches?' asked Liz.

Both boys nodded.

'Okay, then let's go.' Kevin steered them out the door. It had been a stroke of genius for Kevin to turn up in a squad car – Liz knew she'd have had a battle to get them school otherwise. She heard the squad car door slam, and then blue light strobed through the kitchen window as they reversed back down the street – without sirens.

Liz tidied the kitchen. Niall was already at college, but had promised to be back by lunchtime. She knew that Nelson would be all right on his own until then. In spite of her curiosity, Liz was regretting her promise to take Dora to York. She really should have told Kevin about the papers they'd found. At the end of the day, however, it was Dora's call, and Liz knew Dora would never speak to her again if she told Kevin everything. Perhaps that might not be such a bad thing...

A knock at the door interrupted Liz's thoughts. She opened it, expecting Dora, but it was Benedict, with a huge bunch of cream roses.

'For you,' he said.

'Is it my birthday? They're lovely.' They were, each one a delicate parchment colour and shaped perfectly. They couldn't have been easy to find at that time of year.

'I thought I should apologise. For being such a grump. I know it hasn't been easy for you having the boys here.' Benedict took her in his arms. 'Forgive me?'

'Don't be daft. There's nothing to forgive.'

'I'd like to make you a meal tonight, too, if you can manage it? I missed mah-jong yesterday.' They'd had to cancel mah-jong because there was no one to look after the boys.

'Shouldn't be a problem. I think Niall's in tonight.'

They kissed. It gave her a lovely warm feeling, all the way up from her toes to her cheeks.

'Got to dash.' Benedict kissed her nose. 'I've got to get the museum open. See you at seven?'

'At seven.' She waved him out the door.

She was putting the roses in a vase when there was another knock. This time, it *was* Dora.

'Aren't you ready yet? I've taken a day off for this, you know.'

THE DRIVE to York took about an hour and a half, but it seemed much, much longer. She and Dora sat in awkward silence for the first ten minutes, until Liz suggested they put the radio on; then they'd spent the next forty minutes squabbling over which station to listen to. In the end Liz had given in, and so was subjected to Wagner's *Ring* cycle, which put her in an even more jangled mood. Then, on the last leg of their journey, Dora had taken issue with the satnav and had insisted on taking a B road into York that Liz reckoned put at least an extra fifteen minutes on their journey and resulted in the satnav noisily contradicting every single turn they took. Liz was immensely relieved when they arrived on the outskirts of the city.

The address they were looking for lay outside the medieval city walls. Liz was relieved about that. Driving in the heart of York, with its narrow, cobbled streets and one-way systems, could be tricky.

'I think this is it,' said Liz as they turned down a neat Victorian terrace. 'Lower Darnborough Street.'

'*You have arrived at your destination*,' confirmed the satnav.

'About time.' Dora sniffed. 'Which one is it?'

'Number sixty-three. Must be somewhere in the middle.'

They drove past and found it, an unassuming house with a yellow front door. It didn't look in the least bit mysterious.

'What shall we do now?' asked Dora.

Liz gave her a hard look. 'Haven't you thought about that?'

'Not really.'

Liz managed to find a parking spot at the end of the street, and they parked up. They stared at each other in silence for a long minute.

'It's your call, Dora,' said Liz at last, 'although it seems a bit silly to have come all this way without a plan. We should at least knock, don't you think?'

'And say what?'

Liz shrugged. 'Play it by ear.'

'I'm not very good at that kind of thing.'

'Okay, then let me do the talking. I'll just probe, gently, see what the situation is.'

'Probe?'

'Gently.'

Dora thought about that. 'Okay.'

They got out of the car and retraced their steps to the house with the yellow door. Liz knocked. It was opened a few seconds later, by a dark-haired woman in nurse's scrubs, with ferociously plucked eyebrows and bubble gum pink lipstick. Liz judged she was in her late twenties.

'Hello?' she said. 'Can I help you?' She had a Newcastle accent.

'Hello, I was wondering—' Liz began.

Dora cut her off. 'I'm Daniel Holliday's aunt. Who the hell are you?'

Liz didn't know who was most surprised, the dark-haired woman or herself. So much for 'probing gently'!

'Well?' Dora snapped.

All the colour had drained from the woman's face. 'I think you'd better come in.'

She showed them into the front room that faced onto the street. By the neatness of the cushions on the sofa and its faintly dusty air, Liz guessed it was only used 'for best'.

'So?' snapped Dora. 'Who are you, and what are you doing in this house? I have the tenancy agreement in my bag.'

The woman hesitated. 'I'm Dan's wife,' she said. She saw Dora's look of incomprehension. 'His *other* wife.'

There was a stunned beat of silence.

The woman peered at Dora's white face. 'Do you want to sit down?'

Dora dropped onto the sofa.

'You're Amanda, I assume?' said Liz.

The woman nodded. 'Amanda Poulson.'

They heard the front door open.

'Yoo-hoo!' called a woman's voice from the hall. 'It's only me. I couldn't get chai latte, so I just got plain instead.'

Liz's eyes opened wide and met Dora's equally wide ones.

'Where are you?' called the voice.

'In the front room,' answered Amanda. 'I have guests.'

The door was opened clumsily by a woman juggling two takeaway coffee cups. She stood, stunned, in the doorway.

'Oh my God,' breathed Tilly, 'what are you two doing here?'

14

'How did you find me?' asked Amanda. They had all moved to the kitchen, where they now sat around the melamine kitchen table.

'The key,' said Liz, 'that Daniel left with Dora.'

'He told me you would come for it,' said Dora, 'but you didn't.'

Amanda glanced at Tilly. 'No.'

'Was that you in the veil?' asked Liz. 'At the funeral?'

Amanda nodded. 'Stupid idea. I wanted to go, but didn't want anyone to see my face. In the end, it just made people even more curious.'

'Why didn't you come for the key?' asked Dora.

'I wanted the dust to settle first. With Dan dying like that, I didn't want to look suspicious.' Again, Liz saw her glance anxiously at Tilly.

Liz frowned. Amanda had known where the key was, but didn't want to arouse suspicion by coming to get it. So... Liz's eyes widened. Dora's burglary! Had Tilly...? Tilly saw her epiphany on her face and met her appalled look. She shook her head minutely. *Don't go there.*

'How do you two know each other?' asked Liz instead.

'We met as teenagers,' said Tilly. 'We stayed in the same foster home for a while before I went to the YDC.' The Youth Detention Centre, where she'd been sent for habitual breaking and entering. 'We lost touch until we bumped into each other in Middlesbrough in November. I never met Daniel.'

'But you knew he had two wives?' asked Liz.

'No.' Tilly frowned. 'I didn't know that until after he died, and Amanda confided in me.'

Liz turned to Amanda. 'So you knew?'

'I only found out a couple of weeks before he died. I thought he was away on business, and took a drive to Whitby. I saw him and Catriona together. I thought at first it was just an affair.' Her eyes welled with tears. 'I wish it had been. But when I confronted him, he told me the truth... he said it was a relief, after all these years, to get it off his chest.'

'Off his chest?' squeaked Dora. 'I hope you bloody boxed his ears!'

'I threw him out.'

'But you didn't go to the police?' asked Liz.

'I have a daughter. *We* have a daughter. I didn't want to leave her without a name.'

'A daughter?' Dora looked as if any further surprises could finish her off completely.

'Ruby. She's six. She's at school just now.'

Dora was silent, digesting the revelation that she had a great-niece.

'I asked Dan for the house lease,' continued Amanda. 'It's in his name. But he wouldn't give it to me. I think he was hoping I'd change my mind and forgive him. But some things...'

'Unforgivable,' said Dora. 'Bloody unforgivable. If I could get my hands on him, I'd kill him all over again.'

'He told you he'd given the key to Dora?' prompted Liz.

'He said that if anything happened to him, I had to go to Anchor Cottage in Whitby and ask for an envelope with my name on it. Then take it up to plot twelve at Cholmley allotments.'

'Did he think something might happen to him?'

Amanda shook her head. 'I don't think it was that. It was just somewhere to hide his identity papers where Catriona wouldn't find them. And he knew if something did happen to him – something unexpected – I would be left high and dry.'

Liz wasn't completely convinced. 'Did he seem worried to you at all, or scared?'

'I don't know. I didn't care, to be honest. I was just so bloody mad at him. I'm still mad at him.' Amanda sobbed. 'I'm glad he's dead.'

'You don't mean that, Manda.' Tilly put her arm around Amanda's shoulders. That was enough to push Amanda over the edge. She broke down, sobbing in Tilly's arms.

'I think we should go,' said Liz.

'Yes.' To Liz's surprise, Dora agreed. 'For now.' She wagged a finger sternly at Amanda. 'But I will be back.'

THEY SAT MOSTLY in silence on the drive back to Whitby. Their visit to York hadn't turned out at all how Liz had expected. She'd thought they would discover that Daniel was involved in some kind of illegal activity, probably connected to the Nethergates, but not that he had a whole other second life and family. Even in Dora's wildest dreams, she couldn't have guessed she had a great-niece. The shock had knocked her speechless, for which Liz was truly thankful.

It wasn't until they'd got back to Whitby and were getting out of the car that Dora eventually broke her silence.

'Well, I'm glad that's sorted out.' She straightened her clothes.

'Sorted out?' echoed Liz.

'Yes. Done and dusted.'

Liz didn't know what to say. Could Dora really think that was the end of the matter?

'There's no need for you to involve yourself in Daniel's business anymore, is there?'

'I didn't involve myself. You involved me. And I really think you should tell the police about all this.'

'Why? So they can poke their nose into family business and make Catriona a laughing stock? I don't think so.' Dora glared at Liz. 'You're not going to tell anyone, I hope?'

'Not if you don't want me to.'

'I should think not.' She pointed a bony finger at Liz. 'If you do, I swear you'll regret it.' With that final threat, she stomped off across the car park.

Liz watched her go. As far as she was concerned, the matter was far from over – it only deepened the mystery as to how and why Daniel had been killed. Had he really given the key to Dora 'just in case' something happened to him, as Amanda believed? Or had he suspected someone was after him? Dora might not want to tell the police about Daniel's secret family, but Liz knew that kind of secret had a habit of coming out anyway – whether you wanted it to or not.

'DORA'S BURGLAR, I ASSUME?' Liz had given Tilly a couple of hours to get back from York and then had gone to the café to confront her.

'Shhh, keep your voice down.' Tilly cast an anxious look towards the kitchen and pulled Liz to a table in the café window. 'Mags would bloody kill me.'

'I wouldn't blame her. It was a hell of a risk to take, Tills.'

Tilly sighed. 'Manda's an old friend. I couldn't not help her out, could I?'

'Mmm.' Liz was sceptical. Tilly had given up her life of crime – supposedly – but Liz knew she missed the thrill.

Tilly scowled at Liz. 'Don't be such a hypocrite. You're quite happy for me to do *you* a favour when you need it.'

'Point taken.' It was true. Tilly had accompanied her when she'd broken into Chapel Antiques the summer before, and although they hadn't actually stolen anything, they had made a very important discovery. 'I'm still not sure why you both thought a burglary was necessary.'

'Manda really didn't want to come to anybody's attention, especially with Daniel dying the way he did.'

'You might have told me what was going on.'

'I had no idea you were involved, did I? I didn't know Dora had told you about the key.' Tilly grinned slyly at Liz. 'I have to say you make a lovely Holmes and Watson. Which of you is which?'

'Very funny,' said Liz sourly, but then she couldn't stop a smile leaking through. 'I'm surprised you had to ask. I'm Sherlock.'

'Of course you are. I assume it was you who made the brilliant deduction about the allotment?'

'It took me a while to get there. We could have saved ourselves a lot of bother, couldn't we, if we'd confided in each other?'

'We could. Lesson learned.'

'Does Manda have any idea how Daniel died?'

'No. I know she said she's glad he's dead, but people say all kinds of shit when they're grieving. She's heartbroken, really.'

'It must be very hard for her.'

'It doesn't help that her legals are all over the place. Daniel did have life insurance, but if she makes a claim, it'll be fraudulent. Do you think you can persuade Dora to give her the lease and stuff?'

'I think so. I'll blackmail her if I have to.' She caught Tilly's look of surprise. 'I've done it before.'

Tilly grinned. 'And you have the cheek to tell *me* off.'

The bell on the door tinkled. Kevin spotted them as he came in, and came to their table.

'Just grabbing a coffee before I pick the boys up.'

Liz looked at her watch, surprised. The day had flown.

'You want to drink it here,' asked Tilly, 'or takeaway?'

'Takeaway, please.'

Tilly went to prepare his coffee. Kevin sat down opposite Liz.

'Penny for them,' he said.

'Sorry?'

'You're lost in your own little world. What are you thinking about?'

'Oh. Nothing much. Stuff.'

Kevin raised an eyebrow.

'Gryzna. The boys. Daniel Holliday.'

Kevin frowned. 'Why Daniel Holliday?'

'Dora's still very upset.'

'Since when were you worried about Dora Spackle?'

'I'm not. Not exactly. But...' Liz didn't know how to finish that sentence. 'I don't suppose you've found any more about Daniel being in debt?'

'We've spoken to Hermione Nethergate, but we couldn't get any straight answers.'

'You think she's loan sharking?'

'If I had to put money on it, I'd say she was. She actually owns a sixty per cent share of the *Stella Mae*. I think she probably took it as collateral until Masterson repaid the money for the refurb. But we can't really prove that, or press it any further, without actual evidence.' Kevin frowned. 'I find it hard to believe she'd arrange to have Daniel killed just because he owed her money.'

'Really? If she's anything like her husband, she's a tough nut.'

'Yes, but dead men don't pay their debts.'

That was true. Perhaps they *were* barking up the wrong tree.

'Here you go.' Tilly reappeared, with a takeaway cup for Kevin. 'Two shots, as usual.'

'Perhaps I should've asked for three.' Kevin grimaced. 'With the boys, I need all the energy I can get.'

Liz was back at Gull Cottage when Kevin arrived with the twins about three-quarters of an hour later. She was startled to see that Eryk's school shirt was covered in dried blood – he'd managed to cut his hand in the playground. She cleaned the wound as best she could, redressed it, then put his shirt in the washing machine. After that it was a whirlwind of tea, Nelson walking, and reluctant homework. When Niall arrived home, full of tales about his day at college, Liz started cooking for them both.

It was only when she sat down at the table and put the first spoonful of food in her mouth – the first thing she'd had to eat all day – that she saw the roses on the sideboard.

She'd completely forgotten about dinner with Benedict.

15

The next morning, Liz bumped into Mike Howson as she was heading towards the abbey steps for their morning walk.

'Morning, Liz. Wotcha, Nelson.' He bent to rub Nelson's ears.

'I see you have a full complement of fish today?' said Liz. His trolley was filled with herring for the smokehouse.

'Aye. The *Ocean Star* had a good day yesterday. I'll be glad when the *Stella Mae*'s back in action, though.'

'Any idea when that's likely to be?'

'Any day now, the skipper says.' Mike hesitated and rubbed his red cheeks. 'Actually, I'm glad I bumped into you. I was wondering if you could do me a favour.'

'Of course.'

'I'm worried about Catriona. She's not going out at all or even speaking to anyone much. I think she thinks everyone's forgotten about her.'

Liz could sympathise with that. After Mark had died, the world had gone on turning as usual for everyone except her. It was easy to think nobody cared.

'How can I help?'

'I was wondering if you might pop in to see her.'

'Me?'

'You have a way with people.'

'But I don't really know her, Mike. Not that well, anyway.'

'She needs to see a friendly face. It couldn't hurt, could it?'

'I suppose not.' Liz was doubtful, but she liked Mike and didn't want to disappoint him. 'Okay, of course I'll do it. I'll call in this morning.' Now that the twins were at school, she had a little more time to herself during the day.

'That's good of you.' Mike looked relieved. 'You know where she lives, don't you?'

Liz nodded. 'I'll pop into your shop after, if you like, and let you know how she is.'

'Don't worry about that. I can catch you tomorrow morning.' He left her with a wave. 'See you then.'

AFTER A GUSTY WALK in St Mary's graveyard, Liz hurried home and settled Nelson in his basket. He looked at her accusingly when he realised she was going out again without him. She kissed his nose.

'I'm sorry. I know I haven't been around much lately. I'll make it up to you, I promise.'

That would be relatively easy – a few extra walks and a chop would keep Nelson happy. It wouldn't be quite so easy to make it up to Benedict, however. When she'd called him the night before, he'd been very gracious about her having forgotten their dinner date. A little too gracious, in fact. Distant, even. Liz was aware a gulf had opened up between them, but had no idea how to close it again.

It was her own fault. She was simply trying to juggle too many balls, what with the twins, her love life, the holiday lets, the renovation of Benbow Cottage, and Daniel Holliday. The obvious ball to drop was Daniel – his life and death was really none of her business. But somehow, she couldn't do it. She had no idea why his death had got under her skin so much. She wondered whether her mildly obsessive behaviour was what psychologists called 'displacement activity' – was she so preoccupied with Daniel Holliday's life because she couldn't, or wouldn't, face up to problems in her own? It was possible. She'd been trying very, very hard not to think about poor Gryzna or the terrible consequences if she was deported. She'd also been wilfully ignoring a growing discomfort with her relationship with Benedict. It was perfectly natural, surely, after the honeymoon period had passed, to have some doubts and reservations? She'd been on her own so long, she'd lost touch with the etiquette involved in a relationship, with the give and take required to maintain one day in, day out. It was all quite exhausting.

She called in at the baker's on her way to Catriona's, half hoping to see Juliette there, but there was no sign of the Frenchwoman in the busy queue. Liz wondered whether she should call in to see her after she'd seen Catriona. Then she scolded herself. Juliette needed friends her own age, and it was really up to her to make the effort to find them. Liz couldn't make them for her.

After the baker's, Liz headed for the west side of town. The swing bridge was up, so she had to wait with the other pedestrians as a cruiser passed slowly through, on its way to the marina. The bridge inched closed, the barriers went up, and a bell rang to say it was safe to cross. Everyone who'd been waiting hurried off across the bridge. It was only a minute's walk from there to Catriona's flat on New Quay Road.

It took a long time for Catriona to open the door. At first Liz thought she might be out, but then she remembered Mike saying that she never went out, so she was patient and waited.

Eventually Catriona cracked the door open. She was still in her dressing gown and slippers.

'Mrs McLuckie?' She was clearly astonished to see her there.

'Hello. I was wondering how you were, Catriona. I brought you some cake.'

'Oh.' The young woman cast an anxious look back over her shoulder, into the flat. 'That's very kind of you.' She took the cake box from Liz.

There was a very awkward pause.

'Would you like to come in?' Catriona's tone told Liz she'd rather she didn't, but Liz had promised Mike she would check on her, so she ignored it.

'That would be lovely. Thank you.'

Catriona led Liz awkwardly through to the kitchen, a small room at the back of the flat. 'Would you like some tea or coffee?'

'Tea would be lovely, thanks.'

'Sorry about the mess.' There were dirty dishes piled in the sink, and the countertops were littered with empty take-away cartons and a few empty wine bottles. Liz tried not to frown. She really hoped Catriona wasn't looking for comfort in a bottle.

'How are you?' she asked.

'Oh. Fine. I suppose.' Catriona splashed a couple of mugs under the cold tap to clean them. 'I suppose I'm just getting used to... things being different.'

Liz couldn't help but notice that one of the mugs still had pink lipstick on it. She hoped Catriona would give her the other one. As Catriona was putting the kettle on, there was a muffled 'thump' from somewhere else in the flat. It seemed to come from one of the rooms on the other side of the hallway. A bedroom, Liz assumed.

Catriona's eyes widened in alarm that she quickly tried to hide. 'It's just the cat... She's a bit overweight.'

Liz looked at her. She wasn't a good liar.

Catriona broke eye contact and turned back to the teacups. 'Do you take milk?' she asked. 'I'm not sure I have any.'

Liz stood up, with a smile. 'You know what?' she said. 'I don't want to put you to any bother. I'll just leave the cake with you.'

Catriona did her best, but couldn't disguise her relief.

'If you need anything,' said Liz, 'anything at all, you know where I am.'

'Thank you.'

She couldn't get Liz out the door fast enough.

On her way home, Liz pondered her strange visit. She didn't think Mike needed to worry about Catriona being lonely – she had a 'cat' to keep her company.

LIZ CALLED into the café on her way home. Iris and Dickie were there, eating scones, and Tilly was busy at the coffee machine.

'THERE YOU ARE,' said Iris. 'I WAS BEGINNING TO THINK YOU'D VANISHED OFF THE FACE OF THE EARTH.'

'I've been a bit busy, what with the twins and all.'

Iris nodded. 'BIT OF A HANDFUL, THEM TWO, EH?'

'Just a bit.'

Dickie leaned forward. 'What did you say?'

'SHE SAID THE TWINS ARE A TERRIBLE HANDFUL.'

Liz sighed.

Tilly came over. 'You're out and about early.'

'I've just been to see Catriona.'

'How is she?'

'Better than you'd think.'

'Oh?'

'Let's just say she has a cat. A cat called Billy, I'm betting.'

'Eh?' Tilly's face crumpled in confusion. But Liz realised that Iris was listening, so decided a change of subject was in order. 'Do you have any scones left?'

LIZ HAD ONLY BEEN HOME a couple of minutes when there was a knock at the door. It was a tall woman, with elaborately coiffured red hair and a fur-trimmed cape, who looked like she'd just stepped out of one of the Paris fashion shows. She stared down at Liz through artificially long eyelashes.

'I'm looking for Liz McLuckie.' She had a very cultured accent.

'That's me.'

'We'd like a word. May we come in?' There was a young man behind her – a gym bunny with teeth and a thousand-yard stare. Liz's internal alarm started to jangle.

'I'm busy right now.'

'This will only take a minute, won't it, Alan?' She signalled to the man, who stepped forward and inserted his foot in the door before Liz could slam it shut. He shouldered his way in, followed by the woman. Liz retreated to the other side of the kitchen table. Nelson got out of his basket, hackles up.

The woman looked at him. 'I hope that... thing... doesn't bite.'

Liz's own hackles rose. 'Only when I tell him to.'

'Alan?' The woman signalled to the young man, but before he could make a move towards Nelson, Liz grabbed Nelson's collar.

'I've got him. He'll be fine. What on earth is this about?'

The woman pulled out one of the kitchen chairs and

wiped it with a gloved hand before sitting on it. 'A little bird has told me you're taking an interest in my business.'

Liz frowned. 'Your little bird has it wrong. I have no idea who you are.'

'My name is Hermione Nethergate.'

'And I'm Alan.' The young man's high-pitched voice didn't match his pumped-up physique.

The woman glared at him.

Liz glared at them both. 'I'm sorry, but I still don't know what you're talking about.'

'Do you deny it was you who told the police that Daniel Holliday owed me money?'

Ah. Liz couldn't deny that, so she didn't even try. She could have deflected the accusation and blamed Potsy for being indiscreet, but she didn't want to get him into trouble. That wouldn't be fair.

'You've caused me some considerable inconvenience. I've had to tolerate the police poking into my financial affairs. Very intrusive,' Hermione continued. 'I assume you're also the same Elizabeth McLuckie who gave evidence at my husband's trial?'

Liz couldn't deny that either. Sensing her growing unease, Nelson growled.

Hermione Nethergate eyed him with distaste. 'My little bird also tells me you're leaving Whitby, Mrs McLuckie.'

Liz frowned.

'You're leaving Whitby because the sea air isn't good for your health.'

Liz finally realised what was happening. 'Are you threatening me?'

'Threatening? No, I wouldn't dream of stooping so low. I'm just giving you some friendly advice, as someone who is concerned for your well-being.'

'I don't think you know me very well, Mrs Nethergate. Threats don't work. Your husband could tell you that.'

'I don't think *you* know *me*, Mrs McLuckie. Like I said, I don't make threats. If you don't leave Whitby within a week, I guarantee your health will take a turn for the worst. Your health, and the health of the' – her eyes rested malevolently on Nelson – 'things... you care about.'

Nelson barked. Not his usual jolly yip, but a full-throated, menacing bark. Liz was barely managing to hold him.

Hermione got to her feet. 'I'm glad we've had this little chat. I hope we understand each other. *Bon voyage.*' She wrapped her cape around her. 'Alan?'

Alan held the door open for her as she sashayed out.

When they'd gone, Liz let go of Nelson. He hurled himself against the door, snarling and barking. It looked like he'd just found himself another nemesis. And so had Liz. Hermione Nethergate was even more chilling than her less-than-charming husband, Phil.

And Liz could tell she'd meant every word she'd said.

16

Liz sat in Benbow Cottage and shivered.

She was waiting for a delivery of two vintage leather chairs she'd found on an online auction site. They cost more than Irwin had budgeted for, but she'd persuaded him the extra expense would be worth it in the long run. The leather would only improve with wear, unlike almost anything else, which would have to be replaced much sooner. It was easy to underestimate the wear and tear involved with a holiday let.

There was no heating on in the cottage, so Liz sat bundled in her overcoat, sipping on tea she'd brought with her in a flask, warming her feet on Nelson... and thinking about the threats Hermione Nethergate had made the day before.

Liz had no intention of leaving Whitby. She felt at home here and had made many good friends. Plus, she couldn't leave the twins high and dry – that would mean they'd probably have to go back into care. And, of course, there was Benedict. As unsure as she was as to whether they had a future together, she did at least want to give their relationship the best possible chance. He was bound to take it personally if she just upped and left without any explanation, like Gillian Garraway had.

Who was it said 'the best form of defence is attack'? Shakespeare? Whoever it was, they had a point. Could Hermione Nethergate have anything to do with Daniel Holliday's death? If so, and if Liz could prove it, that would solve her problem. But really, there was no evidence that pointed in that direction apart from the fact that Daniel owed Hermione money, which was tenuous at best.

Shakespeare had another saying, of course – '*the better part of valour is discretion.*' And he had a point with that one, too. Maybe she should just keep her head down and hope that everything would blow over?

BANG, BANG.

Liz flinched at the knock at the door. Nelson jumped to his feet.

It was Mike Howson in his high-vis gear, accompanied by Potsy Potter.

'Mrs Mac,' he said, his red face creased with concern. 'Niall said I'd find you here.'

'Sorry, Mike, I forgot I promised to let you know about my visit to Catriona.' Naturally, she wasn't going to say anything about Billy the cat.

Mike shook his head. 'That's not it. You need to come back to Gull Cottage, pronto.'

'Why?' A myriad of possibilities whirled through Liz's head. Another fire? The twins? She'd taken them to school herself that morning, and they'd seemed to be behaving themselves.

'I think you'd best come and see.'

Liz collected her things and Nelson and accompanied the two men up the street. Whatever it was she had to deal with, she hoped she could sort it out and get back before the armchair delivery. Potsy caught her eye as they walked.

'I've been helping Mr Howson. Do you like my vest? It's the same colour as my oilskins.'

'Very nice.'

The reason for her urgent summons became apparent as soon as they got to Henrietta Street. Gull Cottage had been vandalised, with a single word sprayed across the front in bright orange neon paint: LEAVE. Dismayed, Liz hurried to examine it. It hadn't been there when she'd set out for Benbow Cottage, so the graffiti had had to have happened at some point in the last hour or so. She put a finger on it, and it came away orange. Still wet.

Mike frowned. 'If we get it off quick, it might be okay.'

Liz hoped so. Gull and Kipper weren't plastered like some of the other cottages in the street, so the paint had been sprayed straight onto stone. She wouldn't just be able to paint over it.

The door opened. It was Niall, carrying a steaming bucket of water.

'I'm so sorry, Liz,' he said. 'I didn't see a thing. I'd have stopped them if I had.'

'Bloody kids,' muttered Mike.

Liz didn't contradict him. It wouldn't benefit any of them to say who'd actually done it, and, knowing how impetuous Niall could be, might even put him in danger.

Potsy and Niall both took a scrubbing brush from the bucket and attacked the letters. To Liz's relief, the hot soapy water seemed to have an immediate effect.

'You don't think Eryk and Lukasz...?' Niall paused in his scrubbing. It wasn't a totally unreasonable suggestion. In ordinary circumstances, the boys would be among the most obvious suspects for any graffiti in the town.

'No.' Liz leapt to their defence. 'Why would they? Besides, they're in school.'

'Well, whoever it was,' said Mike, 'they have some brass

neck. Doing it in broad daylight like this, when anyone could walk past. It makes no sense.'

But, of course, it made perfect sense to Liz.

And something else was also abundantly clear – keeping her head down and hoping the trouble with Hermione Nethergate would blow over really wasn't an option.

WHEN SHE GOT BACK to Benbow, she discovered that the delivery men had left the chairs in the yard. Even though it was a bit slapdash of them, she was relieved they'd done that rather than taking them away again. She manhandled the chairs into the cottage with difficulty – they were heavy and awkward to get through the narrow cottage doorways. When she'd finally wrangled them into position in the kitchen, she dropped thankfully into one.

She needed to think.

She was in serious trouble, and her options were limited. She could tell Kevin about Hermione's threats, but Liz wasn't convinced that would do any good. All the police could do was warn Hermione off, which would just poke the bear.

She could tell Benedict, Tilly and Niall. They might be able to think of a plan together. But... she would potentially be putting them all in harm's way. So that wasn't an option either.

Her only real option was the one she'd thought about earlier – if she could somehow prove that Hermione Nether-gate was involved in Daniel's murder, that would eliminate the threat. But *was* Hermione involved? As Kevin had said, dead men don't pay their debts. On the other hand, it was quite a co-incidence that Hermione was the major share-holder in the *Stella Mae* – Liz believed she was capable of going to extreme lengths to get anything she wanted. Did she want Daniel dead?

A lot of people potentially did – Billy and/or Catriona, Christian Petit, Amanda Poulson, Catriona's father Earl, and even Skipper Masterson. Almost everyone, in fact, who had ever come into contact with him! Of course, only three of those people had had direct access to him the night he died – Billy, Christian and Skipper. Billy and Christian both had motives. Billy was having an affair with Catriona that might pre-date Daniel's death. Christian and Daniel had had a physical altercation only a few days before. How deep did that animosity go? The Skipper didn't seem to have a motive unless he was acting on Hermione's orders. He had lied about where the *Stella Mae* was when Daniel most likely went overboard. Why would he do that if he wasn't trying to cover something up?

It was a conundrum. And she only had a week to get to the bottom of it.

When she got back to Gull, she was glad to see that there was only the faintest trace of the graffiti left. She hoped the weather would do the rest.

Niall had gone to college, leaving a note saying he would be back in time to make tea, so Liz took Nelson for a long walk – over the swing bridge, along the fish quay and up onto the West Cliff, back through the town, then up Salt Pan Well Steps onto the Donkey Path on the East Cliff, past the Cholmley allotments, a couple of laps around the outer wall of the abbey ruins, then back down the 199 steps to Henrietta Street. She was just letting herself back into Gull Cottage, and was looking forward to putting her feet up, when her phone buzzed.

It was a text from Benedict.

FANCY LUNCH?

She replied:

I'LL BRING IT. SEE YOU IN TEN.

She settled Nelson with a bone and headed out again. She called in at the café for sandwiches, coffee and cake, and then made a beeline for the Captain Cook Maritime Museum on Grape Lane.

Dedicated to explorer Captain James Cook, the museum was a narrow building, four storeys high, criss-crossed with wooden beams and filled with seafaring exhibits. Benedict was a trustee and the head curator.

He spotted her as soon as she came in the door, and beckoned her into his office, where he kissed her on the cheek. That was a little disappointing, but Liz supposed they weren't really private – she could see a few visitors milling about in the exhibition room on the other side of the internal window.

Benedict peeked into the carrier bag she'd filled up at the café. 'Prawn. My favourite. Do you want to eat in here or take it out somewhere?'

'Here. It's going to rain, I think.' The office was cosy, warmed by an electric fire, and Liz really didn't fancy going outside in the cold again.

'Hard to believe it's supposed to be spring,' said Benedict.

'Mm.' Liz looked at him with dismay. Really? Were they doing small talk now? She decided to grasp the nettle.

'Listen, Benedict, I'm really sorry about the other night. I'd had such a busy day I just completely forgot I said I'd come for dinner.'

He shrugged. 'Don't worry about it. It doesn't matter.'

Liz was dismayed to see the left corner of his mouth twitch. She was about to challenge him on it when he distracted her with a question.

'Have you been painting again?' he asked. 'What on earth are you painting that colour?'

She saw he was looking at her finger, which was still stained neon orange.

She told him about the graffiti, carefully omitting the word LEAVE from her narrative. But Benedict pressed her on it.

'What exactly was it they sprayed?'

'Just nonsense words. I daresay it made sense to them.' She knew he would find out eventually, probably from Niall, but she really didn't want to get into that discussion at that moment. Benedict was too sharp not to guess the word meant something.

'These prawns are lovely, aren't they?' she said, taking refuge in small talk again.

'Would you like to come for dinner tonight?'

Liz's heart sank. 'I can't. Niall has a shift at the Duke of York. The boys...'

'You could bring them too.'

'They eat much earlier. They'd think I was trying to starve them to death if I made them wait until eight o'clock.'

'I can make it earlier if you like.'

'Niall's already volunteered. He's buying food on his way home.' Liz felt bad about turning him down, knowing he was making an effort. 'You could come to us, though, if you like?'

'Okay.'

'It won't be anything exotic. But we could watch some telly after?'

'Sounds good. What time do you want me?'

'About five thirty? Is that too early?'

'No, that's fine. I'll be there.'

He didn't ask about staying over, which, perversely, was both a relief and a disappointment to Liz. She would have turned him down, but it still galled her to think he might not want to.

17

The novelty of being taken to school in a police car had worn off after a couple of days, so Liz had relented and allowed Eryk and Lukasz to walk to school and back themselves. It was only fifteen minutes, and they could hardly get lost on the way. That afternoon, however, they arrived at Gull Cottage later than usual. Nelson scrambled out of his basket to greet them, and wagged his stumpy tail. Liz resisted the urge to ask the boys where they'd been.

'Don't you want to take your coat off, Lukasz?'

'I'm cold.'

'Okay,' she said. 'I'm sure you'll warm up soon enough.'

Nelson jumped up at Lukasz. Lukasz pushed him away.

'Get off!' he snapped.

Liz frowned and met Niall's eye. Nelson slunk back to his basket. She decided to let Lukasz's uncharacteristic show of grumpiness pass without comment.

'Do you want to watch some TV before tea?' she asked instead.

'No,' said Lukasz. 'We have homework to do.'

'Yes. Homework!' echoed Eryk.

They ran straight up to their bedroom with their school bags.

Niall raised an eyebrow at Liz. 'That's a first.' He was chopping sweet potato wedges, in an attempt to get the boys to eat something other than chips, burgers and sausages.

'Well, I for one am not going to look that particular gift horse in the mouth,' she said.

Nelson was unsettled in his basket, still on his feet, staring up the stairs after the boys. Liz gave him a consoling scratch behind the ears.

'Do you think we should do some naan bread too, just in case?' Niall looked doubtfully at the tray of potato wedges and the pot of chilli on the stove top.

'It might be a good idea.'

'Benedict likes chilli, doesn't he?'

'He loves it.' It was something they'd often made together.

'Is everything okay with you two?'

'What makes you ask?'

Niall shrugged as he chopped. 'We haven't seen much of him lately.'

Liz sighed. 'The boys are a bit of an anti-aphrodisiac, if I'm honest. But we're fine.' She hoped. She cocked an ear. 'They're very quiet up there.'

'Sure, homework isn't usually a noisy occupation, is it now?'

'Hmm.' Liz wasn't convinced.

Niall caught her eye. 'Stop fussing. They're grand.'

TEA WAS something of a mixed success. The boys wolfed down the chilli, but wouldn't touch the sweet potato or the naans, insisting on eating the chilli with slices of white bread instead. Conversation was a little stilted. Benedict's polite inquiries into what the twins had done at school were rebuffed with monosyllabic answers, while Niall's story about one of his fellow students who liked wearing a medieval breastplate to classes was met with world-weary indifference.

Lukasz licked his plate clean. Liz said nothing, knowing she had to pick her battles.

'Can we have a bath?' he asked.

'A bath?' Liz was wrong-footed. It usually took hours of persuasion to get either of the boys to undertake any kind of hygiene maintenance. 'Um, yes... of course you can.'

When the table had been cleared, Niall headed off to do his shift at the Duke of York, and Liz ran the boys their bath.

She hesitated on her way out of the bathroom. 'Are you sure you wouldn't like clean pyjamas?'

'No, thank you,' said Eryk.

'Go away.' Lukasz was less polite. 'We need our privacy.'

Liz retreated to the sitting room, where Benedict was flicking through channels on the TV.

'What kind of thing do you fancy?' he asked.

'Nothing too heavy. A documentary?'

'Lost civilizations of Indonesia?'

'Perfect.'

They settled on the sofa together. The documentary was fascinating, about how certain ancient sites in Indonesia showed traces of previous, forgotten civilisations. Liz snuggled closer to Benedict, enjoying his warmth and the weight of his arm around her shoulders. It seemed ages since they'd had any kind of physical contact.

Half an hour passed before Liz looked at her watch. She realised they hadn't heard a sound from the boys.

'Do you want me to go up and check on them?' asked Benedict.

'Do you mind? It's better if you do it. They don't like me disturbing their *privacy*.'

Benedict grinned and headed up the stairs. He was back a minute or so later.

'Liz?'

She looked up from the telly.

'I think you'd better come up and see this.'

She followed him upstairs to the bathroom. It took her a moment to realise what it was she was supposed to be looking at. The boys were sitting on the floor, wearing only towels and mutinous expressions. There were assorted other wet towels and clothes strewn about, and a lot of water puddled on the tiles. In the bath, bobbing on the surface of the water with the bubbles, was a fluffy yellow duckling.

'Oh my God.'

'They got it from the petting zoo at Pannet Park, apparently,' said Benedict.

'It was lonely. It wanted to come home with us.'

Liz was – quite literally – speechless. She looked at Benedict and saw he was actually trying to smother a grin. She glared at him, and he straightened his face.

'Can we keep it?' pleaded Eryk.

'Please? It's nice and clean now.'

'Oh my God. Have you *shampooed* it?' There were traces of foam on the duckling's fluff. 'You can't shampoo a duck. You might poison it.'

'Poison it?' Eryk's face crumpled.

Benedict hurried to interject, 'It looks fine to me.' Liz had to admit the duckling did seem perfectly happy, paddling around the tub, peeping gently to itself.

'Can we keep it?' repeated Eryk.

'Please?'

Liz shook her head.

'Why not?' said Lukasz. 'You have a pet. Why can't we have one?'

'Because ducks aren't domesticated animals. And it belongs to someone else.'

'Zoos are cruel,' said Eryk.

'Not all of them.' She took a hand towel from the floor and tried to catch the duckling in it. 'I don't know what they're going to say. They could press charges.'

Lukasz opened his mouth, but before he could speak, Liz forestalled him.

'I've told you before, haven't I? Borrowing without asking is stealing. Which is illegal. You could be arrested.' She could feel tears pricking the backs of her eyes.

'Liz...' Benedict's tone was gentle, but held a note of warning.

Liz felt a flash of anger. She ignored Benedict and turned back to the boys. 'Get dried and put your pyjamas on.'

She carried the duckling downstairs in the towel. Nelson greeted her at the bottom of the stairs with a frustrated whimper. No wonder he'd jumped up at Lukasz when he'd come home from school – Lukasz must have had the duckling tucked inside his coat.

Benedict joined her, his mobile phone to his ear. He shook his head. 'There's no one at Pannet. They must've all gone home for the night.' He looked down at the duckling in the towel and put an arm around Liz's shoulders. 'Cute, isn't it?'

She shrugged him off. 'Why didn't you back me up?'

'I did back you up.'

'No, you didn't. You just stood there, smirking.' Even as she said the words, she knew she was being unfair. She couldn't really say why she was so infuriated, but she was dangerously close to tears.

Two pairs of bare feet thumped down the stairs.

Lukasz, now in his pyjama bottoms, glared at Liz from the bottom step. 'I want to go home,' he cried. 'I hate you.'

Eryk nodded. 'I hate you, too. And you smell like cheese!'

LIZ WOKE the next morning to an empty bed and the bitter taste of defeat. She didn't think she could handle the boys much longer, but couldn't imagine letting them go back into care, either. At least she didn't have the duckling to deal with – Benedict had taken it home with him and had promised to call Pannet Park first thing. If anyone could take the heat out of the situation and persuade the zoo not to press charges, it was Benedict. She knew she'd been unfair to him. The whole situation *was* funny, or at least it *would* have been if there hadn't been so much at stake. If the police got involved, the boys would end up in Middlesbrough again for sure. Liz had never imagined that she'd find them so difficult to look after, or that they'd test her patience so much. She clearly wasn't cut out for motherhood. That thought made her feel even sadder and more inadequate. It was a real effort to get out of bed, but she knew she had no choice if she was to have any chance of getting the boys to school in time.

They went, surprisingly, with minimal fuss. When she waved goodbye to them at the school gate, they went inside without looking back at her. Liz heaved a sigh of relief at the knowledge that they couldn't get into trouble for another six hours, until Niall picked them up.

She was walking back along Church Street when she heard the familiar rattle of trolley wheels behind her. She turned.

'Morning, Mike.'

He was trundling his trolley in the same direction, towards Henrietta Street and the smokehouse. They fell into step together.

'You're a bit late this morning, aren't you?' she said. She saw his stricken expression. 'Is everything okay?'

'Not really. DI Flint has just taken our Billy in for questioning.'

'What?'

Mike ran a rough hand over his cheeks. 'I don't know what to do.'

'Would a cup of tea help at all?'

He just looked at her.

'And a sympathetic ear?'

HE CALLED into Gull after he'd delivered his herring to the smokehouse.

'I don't really have time for tea,' he said as he sat at the kitchen table. 'I need to get back to the shop.'

'A two-minute tea break can't hurt. You look done in.'

'Aye. I am, if I'm honest.' His usually open and friendly face was etched with lines of anxiety. 'I can't stop thinking about the lad, up there at the station.'

'When did they take him in?'

'First thing. They came for him while I was at the fish market. Our Lesley's beside herself.'

'She must be. Do you have any idea why Flint's taken him in?'

He scowled. 'Bloody gossip. You can't even fart in this town without someone finding out and calling it a hurricane.'

Liz almost smiled. That was definitely the pot calling the kettle black. Mike was the biggest gossip in Whitby, but it was never malicious, and stemmed from his genuine interest in people.

'Gossip about what?' she asked.

'Word's got around that Billy and Catriona are' – he searched for the right words – 'having a fling.'

'Are they?'

'Of course not.' Mike pulled a scornful face. 'They've been

friends since primary school. Our Billy has a lass in Sand-send. Debbie. Nice lass. He's been over at Catriona's quite a bit – him and Debbie. Helping her out. Someone's just got the wrong end of the stick.'

Liz cringed. She'd only seen Billy coming out of Catriona's flat once, and then had jumped to conclusions when she'd heard someone in the bedroom. There definitely had been *someone* in the bedroom – Catriona was a terrible liar – but it wasn't necessarily Billy. Liz remembered Iris's avid expression when she'd overheard her talking to Tilly about Catriona and Billy in the café, and a terrible thought occurred to her. Could *she* herself be the source of the gossip? Iris wasn't known for her discretion. What if Flint had somehow heard about it and made Billy her number-one suspect? It was horrible.

Mike saw her appalled expression and misinterpreted it. 'Our Billy will be okay. He's a tough nut. And the police can't have any real evidence against him.'

Unless he actually *was* involved in Daniel's murder. But that didn't seem to be on Mike's radar at all. He was looking at her speculatively.

'You're friendly with that Detective Ossett, aren't you?'

'Yes.'

'Do you think you could have a word? See what's going on? Me and Lesley would be really grateful.'

Liz nodded. It was the least she could do.

KEVIN COULDN'T SPARE the time to talk to her until later that afternoon. They met in their usual spot in the shelter on the West Cliff.

'No Nelson today?'

'No.' Liz had left him at home. The weather was still unpleasant – squally and wet, with a ferocious wind blowing in across the North Sea. 'I do have coffee, though.' She pulled the flask from her bag and poured Kevin a cup.

'You're a lifesaver.' He took a sip. 'I don't have long. What was it you wanted to talk about?'

'I hear Flint's taken Billy Howson in for questioning?'

'Mm. She's had him in an interview room all day. Won't let me anywhere near him.'

'But you know why she's brought him in?'

Kevin cast her a sideways look. 'I do.'

'Because she thinks he's having an affair with Catriona Holliday.'

He nodded. 'You have to admit it doesn't look good. Billy had the motive and the opportunity to kill Daniel.'

'The thing is... I don't think they *are* having an affair.'

'Do you know that for sure?'

'Not for sure, but...' Liz steeled herself. 'I think I might have been the source of the gossip.'

'You?'

'I jumped to conclusions. And didn't keep them to myself.'

'Ah.'

'I feel awful about it.'

He saw her crestfallen expression and hurried to reassure her. 'If Billy and Catriona aren't an item, and Billy has nothing to do with Daniel's death, you don't need to worry. Flint will have to let him go. She can't find evidence that doesn't exist, can she?'

'Mmm.' Liz was doubtful. She wished she had as much faith in the system as he clearly had.

He finished his coffee. 'Thanks for that. Sorry to dash, but I'd better get back. You want a lift?'

'No, thanks. I need to clear the cobwebs.'

She really did. Her head was a jumble of confusing thoughts and not-very-nice emotions, including shame and embarrassment. On her walk back to the old town, she nipped into the Howsons' shop on Baxtergate, to tell them about her chat with Kevin. There wasn't much she could say to reassure Mike and Lesley, but they were grateful she'd tried. Then she headed home. By now, the wind was so strong that she struggled to stay on her feet, and by the time she got back to Gull Cottage, her face was numb and her mind blissfully blank. Niall opened the door before she had the chance to put her key in the lock.

'Liz! Thank God you're back.' He ran an agitated hand through his hair.

'Why? What's happened?' She peered behind him into the cottage for a clue, but only saw Nelson gazing back at her.

'The twins have done a runner!'

18

'They told their teacher they were walking home.'

'But they knew you were supposed to be picking them up.' Liz brightened as an idea came to her. 'Perhaps they've gone to Pannet Park? For the duckling?'

'Duckling?' Niall hadn't got home until late the night before, and then had left early for college, so she hadn't had the chance to tell him about their bath time adventures.

'Long story. I'll tell you later. Maybe they just forgot you were picking them up?' She knew she was clutching at straws. It was an hour and a half since school had finished. 'Maybe they've just gone for a walk?'

'That's what I thought. I've been out looking. No sign. Also...' Niall hesitated, unwilling to be the bearer of bad news. 'I've checked the kitchen cupboards, and there's some stuff missing – tins of beans and some pot noodles. Plus, my sleeping bag's gone from the airing cupboard.'

Liz remembered the boys' unusually bulging bags when she'd dropped them at school that morning. She'd put it down to the fact it was gym day. She felt the ground lurch away from her, and closed her eyes.

'Are you okay?'

She nodded, but she was lying. 'We should call Kevin.'

'Are you sure?' Niall frowned. 'If we tell Kevin, he'll be obliged to tell social services, won't he? And if social services get involved, the boys will go back into care for sure.' He checked his watch. 'Look, it's only half past five. Let's give ourselves a couple of hours, see if we can find them. Then we'll call Kevin.'

'Okay.'

'Tills and Mags will be busy in the café. But what about Benedict? I'm sure he'd help.'

'He's in a cycling club race today. He's not even in Whitby.'

Niall sat down. 'We need to think. Put ourselves in their shoes. Where are they going?'

'They've packed for a trip, so they're probably heading out of town.' She had a thought. 'The train station! Let's check there first and see if anyone's seen them.'

'Good idea.' Niall grabbed his coat. 'What about Nelson?'

'We don't know how long we'll be. We'll have to bring him with us.'

THE TOWN'S railway station was only five minutes' walk away, a small Victorian building with just two platforms. When they got there, Liz approached the plexiglass screen at the ticket office.

'Hello. I was wondering if you've seen two boys about ten years old.'

The female clerk eyed her sourly. 'Dark spiky hair, full of cheek?'

'That's them!'

'They got the Middlesbrough train.'

Liz wasn't sure whether to be relieved or outraged. 'You sold them tickets to Middlesbrough? On their own?'

'They were with their grandad. Bought three tickets. All paid for in two- and one-pence pieces. It took me a bloody age to count it out.'

Eryk's poker winnings.

'Did you actually see their grandad?' asked Liz.

'They said he was waiting on the platform.' The clerk saw Liz's accusing expression and crossed her arms. 'It's hardly British Rail's fault, is it, if you let them go wandering about on their own?'

Liz knew there was no point arguing. 'What time's the next train to Middlesbrough?'

'Ten minutes.'

'Two returns, please.'

'The dog's extra.'

They paid for their tickets and headed to the platform.

'What on earth are they going to Middlesbrough for?' asked Niall. 'Surely they're not going back to the care home?'

Liz really hoped not. She knew their experience at Gull Cottage had been less than perfect, but surely it hadn't been *that* bad?

'That can't be it,' said Niall, voicing her thoughts. 'It must be something else.'

Liz gasped. She recalled the meeting they'd had at Benedict's house with Caroline Burlington, where Caroline had told them Gryzna was in a detention centre in Middlesbrough. The door had been ajar, and she'd suspected the twins had been eavesdropping on their conversation. It looked like she might have been right.

Niall saw her look of dawning realisation. 'What?'

'I think I know where they're going.'

. . .

THE TRAIN JOURNEY took an hour and twenty minutes, every second of it torture for Liz. Usually, it was a scenic trip, through the wooded valley of the river Esk, crossing and recrossing the water over a succession of bridges before climbing up onto the bleak, beautiful moorland of the North York Moors National Park. Today, however, Liz and Niall were denied the view because it was dark outside. Condensation trickled down the carriage windows, leaving Liz only her rippled reflection to stare at. Niall, sensing her mood, left her alone with her thoughts.

She would never forgive herself if anything happened to Eryk and Lukasz. She'd been distracted by Daniel's murder and Hermione's threats, when the boys should have been her main priority. And she'd been too harsh with them about the duckling.

Middlesbrough train station was grey and unfriendly, much the same as any of the hundreds of Victorian railway stations all over the country. There was no sign of the boys on either of the platforms or in the booking hall. While Niall went to check the gents' toilets, Liz found a station guard. He hadn't seen the boys, but said he would ask his colleagues and took her mobile number to call her if he had any news.

Liz, Niall and Nelson headed into the rainy night, towards Middlesbrough town centre. Cars and buses swished by them on the main road. Liz tried not to let hopelessness overwhelm her, but it was horrifying to think the boys were out there somewhere on their own. It was like looking for a needle in a haystack.

After ten minutes of aimless walking, Liz stopped under a shop awning. 'This is a waste of time,' she said. 'We don't have any idea where the detention centre is, and neither do they. They could be anywhere.' She looked at her watch. It had been almost two hours since she'd arrived back at Gull Cottage to find them gone. 'I'm going to call Kevin.'

Niall nodded grimly. 'He'll be able to get in touch with the police here and organise a proper search.'

Liz felt tears prickle her eyes. 'We should have called him two hours ago.'

Yip! Nelson gave a delighted bark and started pulling on his lead.

'What's up with him?' asked Niall.

'I think he wants to go this way.'

He was tugging Liz to the left, towards a narrower street that led at right angles to the main street.

'Let's see where he takes us,' said Niall.

They'd only gone a few yards down the street when the smell of cooking hit them.

'He just wants food,' said Liz. 'It's past his dinner time.'

Nelson wasn't the only one. Liz's own stomach gurgled at the delicious, savoury aroma.

They went a couple of dozen yards down the street; then Nelson stopped and scratched at a doorway. It was a café – Café Truva – the lights were on, and the sign said 'open'. Liz tried to peer through the window, but it was impossible to see anything because of the condensation inside.

'What do you think?' she asked Niall. 'Should we go in?'

Niall shrugged. 'Can't hurt. We can have a cuppa and call Kevin.'

The bell gave a deep 'BING BONG' as they went in.

Yip! Nelson made a beeline straight for one of the tables. Eryk jumped off his chair to greet him.

'Nelson!' He threw his arms around him.

Lukasz looked up with a bored expression.

Relief sluiced through Liz. She ran to them and gave them both a hug. 'We've been looking everywhere for you. Why did you run off?' She was too relieved to be really angry.

'We didn't run,' said Lukasz, tolerating her hug with a grimace. 'We walked. Then we got the train.'

'Didn't you think we'd be worried?' asked Niall. 'We've been worried sick.'

Lukasz shrugged. 'We thought you'd be pleased if we brought Mum home.'

Liz didn't know what to say. This wasn't the time or the place to try to explain the intricacies of the British immigration system to the boys. None of it made sense anyway, even to her.

'We ran out of money,' said Eryk. 'So we thought we'd just stay here until you came for us.'

Liz was lost for words again.

The café owner, who'd been listening to the exchange, came over. He was a big man dressed in a striped apron, with an impressive handlebar moustache. 'I asked them why they were on their own, but they wouldn't tell me. I was going to give it another ten minutes, then call the police.'

Lukasz scowled at him.

'We've been showing everyone Mum's photo,' said Eryk. 'But nobody's seen her.'

'Middlesbrough's a big city. It would be a miracle if anyone had.' Liz's stomach growled again. 'Have you had anything to eat?' she asked.

'We've shared a hot chocolate,' replied Lukasz. 'But I'm starving.'

'Me too,' piped Eryk.

Niall chipped in, 'I wouldn't mind a little something. My belly thinks my throat's cut.'

Liz turned to the café owner. 'Can we see a menu, please?'

AFTER THEY'D EATEN, they made their way back to the train station.

'There's a train in twelve minutes,' said Niall, who had consulted his phone. 'I think we'll make it.'

'Not if Nelson doesn't pick up the pace a bit,' said Liz. Nelson was walking much more slowly than he had on the way there, probably because of the amount of food that had been secretly fed to him under the table. The boys had told them all about their adventures while they were eating, and Liz had managed to extract a promise that they wouldn't run off again. She wasn't exactly sure how much that promise was worth.

'I need a wee,' said Lukasz as they arrived in the echoing booking hall. It was a big space with a polished concrete floor, incorporating the external arches of the original Victorian station.

'So do I,' said Niall. 'Come on, both of you. We'll have to be quick.'

He took the boys into the gents' toilets, while Liz and Nelson waited outside.

There were quite a lot of people about, waiting to catch what was one of the last trains of the evening back to Whitby. Two figures entered the hall and caught her eye: a man and a woman. The man was tall, with short hair silvered at the temples. The woman was chic and slender, in a red coat and black leather boots.

Liz ducked instinctively behind a plant display, pulling Nelson after her. The palms didn't offer much in the way of concealment, but Liz needn't have worried – Benedict and Gillian Garraway seemed only to have eyes for each other. Benedict bent his head close to Gillian's and said something that made her laugh. Liz closed her eyes in silent anguish. He'd said he was taking part in a cycling race today, but that had clearly been a lie. When she opened her eyes again, she saw that they had parted company – Gillian heading back out into the rain, and Benedict towards the platforms.

Niall and the boys emerged from the toilets.

'You okay?' asked Niall. 'You look like you've seen a ghost.'

'I'm fine,' she lied. 'Just reaction setting in, I think.' She felt like someone had punched her in the heart.

'I know what you mean,' said Niall. 'I'm feeling a bit shaky myself.' He turned to the boys. 'Come on, you two, get a wiggle on, or we'll miss the train.'

The train was already waiting at the platform. Rather than getting on the nearest carriage, Liz shepherded them all down to the furthest one. She really didn't want to bump into Benedict on the train, although a perverse part of her would have liked to see his face when he realised he'd been caught out. When it came to it, though, she was too much of a coward to risk it.

The journey passed in a blur. When the train arrived at Whitby, Liz pretended she'd lost a glove, to give Benedict time to leave the station before they got off the train. They all walked back to Gull Cottage in the rain, Niall and the boys swapping banter and insults, and Liz nursing her aching heart.

19

The next morning dawned breezy but unexpectedly bright. Liz had told the boys they could take a day off school to recover from their adventures, so she left them and Niall snoring in their beds while she took Nelson for his early morning walk up the abbey steps to St Mary's churchyard.

She stopped on one of the coffin steps halfway up. It really was a beautiful day, with high white clouds scudding across a pale blue sky, and sunlight gleaming off the water in the harbour below. Everything smelled clean, salty and fresh. Springlike, even. But Liz wasn't in the mood to celebrate. She was still thinking about Benedict and Gillian Garraway.

She knew Gillian had taken a position in another North Yorkshire diocese, but didn't know where. Gillian hadn't really been on speaking terms with Benedict when she'd left. She hadn't told him why she'd broken off their relationship so abruptly, or why she was leaving Whitby. Only Liz had known the reason. Although Liz had felt sorry for her, there was a certain amount of relief mixed with her sympathy. At the time, she was only just beginning to acknowledge her own feelings for Benedict.

It was possible that Benedict and Gillian's rendezvous in Middlesbrough was perfectly innocent. But if so, why had he lied about the cycle race?

Nelson, impatient with her lack of forward motion, started to tug on his lead, desperate to get up to the graveyard to chase rabbits. She let him pull her up the rest of the steps. In front of her, in the distance, stood the gaunt ruins of the abbey church. Immediately to her left, on a mound just a few feet away, loomed the Celtic cross of St Caedmon, and beyond that squatted the church of St Mary's, where Daniel Holliday's memorial had been held. Liz dismissed the thought of Daniel – her obsession with his death had caused almost all her current problems, including her trouble with the twins and her issues with Benedict. She should have been concentrating on her own relationships rather than worrying about those of a man she'd never even met.

Liz took the left-hand path and let Nelson off his lead. He shot off, like an ungainly bullet, in search of rabbits. Liz followed more sedately, keeping to the path that skirted around the church, threading the gap between it and the clifftop.

What if Benedict had rekindled his romance with Gillian? Although it was a betrayal, Liz was honest enough to admit she'd been using the twins as an excuse to keep Benedict at arm's length. She loved their physical relationship, but... if she was honest... she was scared of emotional intimacy. She knew that had been frustrating for Benedict. Was it too late to put it right?

Liz paused on the clifftop and took a deep breath of salty air. She looked around for Nelson, but there was no sign of him among the ancient gravestones and wet tussocky grass. She kept walking, around to the other side of the church.

Eventually, she arrived back at St Caedmon's Cross, where she'd started. There was still no sign of Nelson.

Liz whistled. She half expected to see his furry little body hurl itself towards her through the gravestones, but there wasn't even an answering yip. She whistled again.

'Nelson! Here, boy!'

Still nothing. Where on earth had he got to? He was too big, surely, to be stuck down a rabbit hole? Had he somehow wriggled underneath the barbed-wire fence and fallen down the cliff? She did another lap of the church, this time peering over the cliff, down onto Henrietta Street. To her relief, there was nothing to see but a jumble of fallen rock and the roofs of the cottages below. Had he just decided to go home? He'd never done that before. Liz looked about, but there was no one else around to ask if they'd seen him.

She retraced her steps back to St Caedmon's Cross. Now she was seriously worried. She decided to go home and see if he was there, and was just about to start down the steps when she heard a noise – the slam of a car door. She scurried to the pedestrian gate that led into the museum car park. There was only one car there, a black SUV with blacked-out windows. Its engine started just as Liz entered the car park. It revved noisily and shot off towards the main car park gate. As she watched, open-mouthed, the SUV swerved suddenly to the right, then veered violently to the left... and crashed into the gate post.

The driver's door opened, and someone half-fell, half-scrambled out. Even though she was still thirty yards away, Liz recognised Hermione Nethergate's henchman, the gym bunny with teeth. He had an enraged bull terrier attached to his left arm.

'Gerrof!' he howled in pain, trying to shake Nelson loose.

Liz was frozen to the spot. Something shot past her – something huge, grey and hairy – making her jump. In her confused state, she thought for a second it was the barghest, the demon dog of Whitby, but then realised it was a massive Irish wolfhound.

'What in God's name is going on?'

Liz recognised the voice, but had trouble reconciling it with the pastel-coated figure she saw behind her. Skipper Masterson glared at her, perplexed.

'He's trying to steal my dog!' she said. 'Help me, please!'

They both ran towards the struggling man. The wolfhound got there first. It leapt up and put its paws on the man's shoulders, toppling him to the ground. Nelson released his jaws and backed away, yipping and snarling. The wolfhound stuck its snarling snout into the man's terrified face.

Liz managed to grab Nelson's collar. He was covered in blood.

Skipper hauled the man to his feet. 'What in God's name are you up to?' He shook him like a rat.

The young man clutched his arm and howled with pain. Skipper saw the blood and let him go. The man staggered, then scrambled upright and ran for the SUV. He got in, backed away from the gatepost at speed, then shot forward again, out of the gate, smoke belching from the exhaust.

'Is your dog hurt?' asked Skipper.

'I don't know.' On closer examination, Liz couldn't find any wound on Nelson. 'I don't think it's his blood. I think he bit him.'

'No more than the bugger deserves.' Skipper looked at her properly for the first time. 'Mrs McLuckie?'

'Liz.' She nodded. 'Thank you. I don't know what I'd have done if you hadn't been here. You and your dog.'

'That's Griff. He's a big softie, really.'

Now that their tormentor had gone, the wolfhound and

Nelson were getting acquainted, sniffing and circling each other.

Skipper scratched his beard. 'Who would want to steal your dog?'

Liz sighed. 'Hermione Nethergate. I'm afraid I've got on her bad side.'

The name had a startling effect on the big trawlerman. His face drained of colour.

'Not a great place to be,' said Skipper. 'Believe me, I know.'

Liz saw his coat was running with red. 'You have blood all over you,' she said. 'You can't go home like that. Please, let me clean you up.'

GULL COTTAGE WAS STILL quiet when they got there. Liz assumed that was because the events of the night before had worn everyone out, and was grateful for it. She took Skipper's coat off him, revealing a brightly coloured fisherman's gansey underneath. The kitchen suddenly felt a lot smaller with Skipper in it. He filled the space with his big frame, his head almost reaching the beams.

He took a seat while she ran some hot soapy water into the sink and scrubbed at the coat. 'I don't think it's going to stain.'

'I wouldn't worry about it. It's only a bit of blood.'

As she continued to scrub, she studied Skipper from the corner of her eye. His beard and size gave him a forbidding air that prevented casual scrutiny, but his eyes were golden brown, and his skin was tanned, with white lines around his eyes. Was it because he spent so much time in all weathers, she wondered, or were they laughter lines? She tried to work out how old he might be. The first few times she'd seen him, she'd thought he was in his mid- to late fifties, but now she'd looked at him properly, she thought he could be a fair bit younger than that. His beard made him look older.

He caught her staring at him, and gave her a quizzical look.

'So, do you want to tell me what you've done to Mrs Nethergate to get on her bad side?'

'Well, first of all, I gave evidence for the prosecution at her husband's trial. Do you know Phil Nethergate?'

'I do. A tosspot of the first order.'

Liz couldn't argue with that assessment. She continued, 'Then, more recently, I mentioned to the police that Daniel Holliday owed Hermione money. She seemed to think that was none of my business.'

Skipper grinned, revealing strong white teeth. 'And she'd be right.'

'Yes, but—'

'I'm only pulling your leg. How did you find out that Doc owed her money?'

'Potsy told me.'

'Ah. Potsy.'

'He told me that you do, too.'

Skipper pulled a rueful face. 'I borrowed off Phil Nethergate to overhaul the *Stella* last year. Stupid. You'd think I'd know better at my age.'

Again, Liz wondered what age that might be.

Skipper, unaware of her curiosity, kept talking. 'I thought the debt would be cleared when Nethergate went to prison, but his wife thought otherwise. She insisted on taking a share of the *Stella* for the payments I'd missed. Now it looks like I'm going to have to sell her.' He saw Liz's puzzled expression. 'The boat.'

Liz had thought for one comical second he'd meant Hermione. She would sell Hermione if she could. There was a gleam in Skipper's eyes that told her he'd followed her train of thought.

'I'd better get on,' he said. 'The police are releasing the *Stella* this morning. I have to see what damage has been done. Come on, Griff.'

To Liz's surprise, she saw that both dogs had settled in Nelson's basket. The wolfhound slunk regretfully out.

Skipper took his coat from her. 'What are you going to do?' he asked. 'Are you going to report it to the police?'

'I don't think so. I think it might just make things worse.'

Skipper nodded. 'You're probably right.' His expression hardened. 'The woman's a bloody menace. Something needs to be done about her.'

Benedict rang as she was trying to get the blood off Nelson.

'I've just been in the café. Tilly's told me about the boys' bid for freedom.'

Liz had spoken to Tilly on the phone the night before, after they'd put the boys to bed.

Benedict sounded hurt. 'Why on earth didn't you call me and let me know what was going on?'

'I knew you were at your race. I didn't want to distract you.' She hesitated. 'How did it go?'

'Not great. The weather was filthy, and I wasn't even placed. I wish I'd never bothered, if I'm honest.'

She wondered just how honest he was prepared to be. 'See anyone you knew?'

'At the race? It's always the same old faces.'

'I never asked you where it was.'

'Rosebery to Helmsley and back.'

'Did you drive there?'

'No, I took the bike on the train, then rode the rest of the way.'

'You must have been worn out by the time you got there. No wonder you weren't placed.'

He laughed. 'I knew there must be a reason I was so rubbish. How about I bring some fish and chips for tea? The boys like fish, don't they?'

'You might be safer with sausage and chips.'

'Right you are. See you about five thirty. With sausage and chips.'

'Five thirty.' Liz hung up, her heart sore.

20

'I can't believe the difference in here.' Irwin gazed around Benbow Cottage in amazement.

'Sorry, what?' Liz hadn't really been listening. She'd been thinking about Benedict. It had been almost a week since she'd seen him in Middlesbrough with Gillian, and although they'd seen each other a few times since then, she still hadn't plucked up the courage to ask him about it.

'The difference,' repeated Irwin. 'It looks fantastic.'

Liz had to agree. Benbow had been Iris's home for decades, and she'd done virtually nothing to it in all that time. When Liz had agreed to project-manage the renovations, there had been no central heating, the bathroom had had a turquoise suite – a throwback to the 1980s – and the kitchen had been a jumble of ill-fitting cabinets and wonky shelves.

But now Liz was delighted with the transformation. The cottage had efficient gas central heating, neat Victorian-style radiators, and classic white bathroom fittings with duck-egg-blue tongue-and-groove panelling. The kitchen was fitted with Shaker-style base cupboards, and the wonky open shelving had been replaced by neat plate racks that were home to a charming assortment of seaside-themed crockery. An antique scrubbed pine table took pride of place in the middle of the kitchen, ringed by pine chapel chairs. The two leather chairs had found a cosy spot by the fireplace, which now had a new woodburning stove.

She handed the keys to Irwin. 'Colin Tarley's said he's happy to come and take some photos for you. It looks so much better on the letting websites if the photos are professional.' Colin was a freelancer who mostly worked for the *Whitby Bugle*. He'd taken the photos for Kipper and Gull, so Liz knew he'd do a great job.

'That's fabulous. I'll give him a call.' Irwin kissed Liz on the cheek. 'You are a miracle worker.' He eyed her. 'I know you've had your hands full with the boys and their daring bid for freedom.'

'You heard about that?'

Irwin gave a wry chuckle. 'Everyone's heard about it. You know Whitby.'

She did. As Mike had said, when it came to their little seaside town, every fart was a hurricane. Luckily, there had been no repeat of Eryk and Lukasz's fugitive behaviour, for which Liz was thankful.

'I also heard about Nelson,' added Irwin. 'Apparently he put up quite a fight? Did you "*Cry Havoc and let slip the dogs of war*"?' Even though he worked as a mortician, Irwin had a theatrical background that occasionally leaked out.

'Who did you hear that from?'

'A little bird.'

Liz hadn't told anyone about it, knowing that it might prompt some awkward questions from her friends about why exactly she was being threatened by Hermione Nethergate. She hadn't wanted to involve them in a potentially dangerous situation. It seemed, however, that Skipper Masterson hadn't been so tight-lipped. Liz supposed he'd had no reason to be, but she was still surprised – he didn't strike her as someone who would be cavalier with other people's business.

Irwin grimaced. 'That Hermione Nethergate's a nasty piece of work. But I don't think you need to worry too much about her.'

'Why?' Liz frowned. 'What do you mean?'

'You haven't heard?'

'Heard what?'

Irwin just shook his head. 'You'll find out soon enough.'

Liz tried to get him to explain his cryptic comment, but he refused to expand on it, insisting instead that he take her to the Full Moon Café for a celebratory coffee and cake.

Kevin was in the café when they got there, chatting to Tilly at the counter.

'Liz!' he called. 'I have a bone to pick with you.'

'Oh?'

'Why didn't you call me when the boys went missing?'

'Niall and I thought you'd be obliged to tell social services.'

'Mm.' Kevin pulled a rueful face. 'I suppose that's probably true. Maybe it was for the best. It would have put me in a spot. I'm glad it ended well anyway.'

'How's things at the station? Have you been busy?'

'Very.'

Liz resisted the urge to ask him how the *Stella Mae* investigation was going. She knew that Billy Howson had eventually been released without charge. He and Catriona had both sworn they weren't having an affair, which had effectively left him without a motive, and DI Flint without a convincing suspect. Liz hadn't heard whether the forensic investigation had turned up anything suspicious on the *Stella Mae*, but she assumed it hadn't. She was pretty sure she would have heard otherwise. She couldn't imagine any of the crew killing

Daniel. Liz had decided that Skipper hadn't necessarily been lying about being at Sheringham Shoal at midnight on the night Daniel went overboard – he might simply have been mistaken. Now that she knew him a little better, she was inclined to give him the benefit of the doubt.

Which left the million-dollar question – how on earth did Daniel Holliday die?

Liz had to keep reminding herself it was none of her business. She had resolved to stay out of murder investigations in the future and concentrate instead on the twins, getting Gryzna back, and rebuilding bridges with Benedict. Even though Benedict still hadn't come clean about seeing Gillian, Liz wanted them to stay together.

Irwin bought a toastie for himself and a slice of Victoria sponge and pot of tea for Liz. They joined Kevin at the counter to eat.

The door opened, and Benedict came in, as if Liz's thoughts had somehow conjured him. He spotted them and came over.

'I'm glad you're here, Liz. I wanted a word.' He gave her a meaningful look. 'In private?' They found a spare table near the window. He said nothing for a moment or two, as if unsure where to start. 'You've been very distant with me since the boys went to Middlesbrough.'

'Mm?'

'It's only just dawned on me why that might be. I've asked Niall which train you got back that night.' He looked deeply into her eyes. 'Did you see me with Gillian?'

Liz looked away and stared into her teacup, which told Benedict everything he needed to know.

'Why on earth didn't you ask me about it?'

Stung by his accusatory tone, her eyes flashed up at him. 'Maybe I didn't want to hear the answer. Or listen to you lie again.'

He frowned. 'Lie?'

'You weren't at the race.'

'I was. I got the train to Middlesbrough and rode to the race at Rosebery from there. On the way back, I changed at the station, put the bike and my gear in a locker, then went to meet Gillian.'

Liz supposed that was plausible. 'So why didn't you tell me you were meeting her?'

'We haven't been getting on that well lately, and I didn't want to rock the boat. I knew you wouldn't be happy about it.'

Well, that was true. She wasn't.

Benedict continued earnestly, 'Gillian called me and asked if we could meet up. She said that the way she'd ended things between us was playing on her conscience. She wanted to explain.'

'And did she?'

'Yes.'

Liz gave him a searching look, but he gave no indication about what he thought about Gillian's motivations.

'She told me that you knew all about it,' he said. 'That she'd taken you into her confidence... Why didn't you tell me?'

'I couldn't. It wasn't my secret to tell.'

'All this time, you knew why she'd dumped me, and you said nothing.'

Liz searched his face. He didn't look angry. If she was honest, she was having trouble gauging how the conversation was going.

He smiled. 'You're infuriating, you know that?' He leaned forward. 'Infuriating and adorable.'

He kissed her.

Liz was astonished. She wasn't sure whether to be delighted or feel rather patronised. 'Really?'

'Really.'

She watched his lips. There was no sign of a twitch – he was telling the truth.

The bell tinkled again as a new customer came in. Hermione Nethergate was wearing tightly fitting leopard-print trousers and a metallic silver ski jacket emblazoned with Gucci logos. Her gym-bunny shadow was behind her as usual. Liz was disappointed to see that he seemed to have recovered from his dog bite.

Hermione strode to the counter, high heels clacking. 'Two lattes, to go,' she snapped. 'Quickly, please.'

Tilly returned her gaze coolly. 'Our coffee machine's broken.'

Hermione looked at Irwin's and Kevin's coffees on the counter beside them and frowned.

'Okay, I suppose we'll have to make do with tea, then.' She glanced at her henchman. 'Tea alright for you, Alan?'

He nodded, ill at ease.

Tilly shook her head. 'I can't do tea either. We've run out of teabags.'

Hermione's eyes narrowed. She looked at the chiller behind the counter, where canned drinks were clearly visible. 'I'll take two Cokes, then.'

'We don't have any.'

'I can see them right there.'

'They're just dummies. For display.'

'Dummies?' Hermione put her hands on her hips. 'I really don't think so.' She turned to glare around the café like a furious Medusa, intent on turning everyone to stone. Her crimson lips drew into a snarl. 'If that's the way you all want to play it, so be it. Tell them, Alan. Explain to them the conse-quences of tangling with me.'

Alan stared at her for a long moment, then shook his head.

'You know what,' he said, in his high-pitched voice. 'I don't think I will.' He laid a set of car keys on the counter beside her. 'It was bad enough helping you put the screw on people, but dogs? Nah. I'm not a dognapper. You can drive yourself home.' He strode out, leaving Hermione staring after him. To her credit, she recovered her composure pretty quickly.

'He's a fool,' she declared. 'You're all fools.' She headed out of the café herself. She was halfway to the door when she realised she'd left her car keys on the counter and had to retrace her steps to get them. Her face flamed. 'Fools!' she declared for a final time before going out and slamming the door behind her.

'Very well done, Tilly!' said Irwin. He clapped as Tilly did a little curtsey.

Liz blinked. 'What on earth was that about?'

'Haven't you heard?' said Benedict. 'Hermione Nethergate's been sent to Coventry.'

Irwin, Kevin and Tilly came to join them.

'It's marvellous, isn't it!' Irwin could hardly contain his excitement. 'The whole town's turned against her.'

'The whole town?' repeated Liz.

'Every shop, restaurant and café,' confirmed Tilly. 'Everyone's had enough. We've all agreed not to serve her. She can't buy so much as a loaf of bread or carton of milk. She even has to go to Sandsend to get petrol.'

'Mum tells me her cleaners have quit too,' said Irwin.

'And,' continued Tilly gleefully, 'the council aren't emptying her bins. I've also heard that her planning application for her new garage is going to be turned down.'

'Wow,' said Liz.

'That's not even the best of it.' Kevin grinned.

'No?' said Irwin. 'What else? Do tell!'

'We got a call from her at the station first thing. Someone

dumped a load of fish heads on her driveway last night. About half a ton of them.'

'Phew! That must stink!' crowed Tilly.

'To high heaven,' agreed Kevin. 'No one's been to see her, though. We're in no particular hurry to get involved.'

Fish heads? A light was beginning to dawn for Liz. 'Who started all this, do you know?'

Irwin glanced around with a conspiratorial air. 'Not officially, but I think we all have a pretty good idea.'

Liz opened her mouth, about to voice her suspicions, when Tilly forestalled her, a finger to her lips.

'Shhhh! Loose talk costs lives. We're all in this together.'

Liz closed her mouth again.

It seemed that Whitby had its very own Scarlet Pimpernel.

AFTER SHE'D FINISHED her cake, Liz walked Benedict back to the Captain Cook Museum. They kissed goodbye in the doorway – not just a perfunctory peck on the lips, but a proper kiss that made Liz feel like a teenager again. Her lips were still tingling as she headed for the fish quay.

All the crime scene tape had gone from the *Stella Mae*. She spotted Skipper on deck, winding rope, his big legs braced against the rise and fall of the boat as it rode the swell in the harbour. Griff was fast asleep on the deck beside him. She looked down at him over the quayside railings. He stopped winding when he spotted her.

'Hello!' She waved.

'Hello!' He looked up at her with a grin.

'I was wondering if I could have a word,' she called. 'Can you come up?'

His grin widened. 'Why don't you come down?'

Liz looked doubtfully at the flimsy metal ladder. It didn't

look as if it could take her weight. But then she rationalised that if Skipper had used it, it must be okay. It took a bit of manoeuvring to get onto the top rungs, as the ladder was vertical to the quayside wall, but once she was actually on it, it was easy enough to climb down.

'That's it. I've got you.' Skipper put his hands on her waist to steady her as she stepped onto the boat. The boat rose up to meet her foot unexpectedly, and she mis-stepped. Skipper's grip tightened. 'There you go.'

Liz flushed. She could feel the motion of the deck beneath her feet, an odd sensation. It was just a gentle swell today – God knows what it must be like in a storm.

'I didn't think you would actually do it,' said Skipper.

'Never dare a fool.' She had to admit she was quite pleased with herself.

'What was it you wanted a word about?'

'Hermione Nethergate.'

'Ah.' Skipper frowned.

'Was it you who instigated the rebellion against her?'

'I have no idea what you're talking about.' But the gleam in his eyes told her otherwise.

'Thank you. Hopefully, it'll distract her from her vendetta against me and keep Nelson safe. But...'

Skipper looked at her expectantly. His eyes really were a striking colour – golden tawny brown, like a lion's.

'But...?' he prompted.

She struggled to regain her train of thought. 'But won't it cause problems for you? With the *Stella Mae*?'

He shrugged. 'It can't make things any worse. I have to sell anyway.'

'Really?' Liz was dismayed.

'There's no way round it. Having the *Stella* out of action for so long was the nail in my coffin. Money-wise.'

'I'm sorry.'

'Me too.'

'What will you do?'

'Crew on another boat, I suppose. In Grimsby or Hull.'

'Leave Whitby?'

'I don't have much choice. The *Ocean Star* is fully crewed. Still, it could be worse.' He smiled. 'There's always tea. Would you like some?' He laughed at her look of surprise. 'It's not a Viking longship. We do have a galley.'

Tempted as she was, she had to get back to Nelson. 'I've just had some, thanks.'

'Another time, then.'

'Another time.' She nodded, then eyed the ladder.

'Don't worry,' he said. 'It's easier going up than coming down.'

'Glad to hear that.' Liz smiled. 'Thanks again for your help with Nelson. And with Hermione.'

'No problem. That's what we do in Whitby. We look after each other.'

21

Liz pulled the duvet back over her shoulders and tried to go to sleep. She'd been lying awake for a couple of hours, desperately counting sheep, but it wasn't working. Normally, she would have put the light on and read for a little while until she nodded off, but she couldn't do that because she didn't want to disturb Benedict. She had finally relented and let him stay the night. As he'd said, he was hardly a stranger to the twins, and she didn't want to put her love life on hold indefinitely. She didn't know how much longer it would be until Gryzna was released. Caroline Burlington was hopeful it wouldn't be too much longer, but Liz wasn't holding her breath.

It wasn't Gryzna who was keeping Liz awake, however.

It had been a couple of days since her daring descent down the ladder onto the *Stella Mae,* but for some reason Skipper's words kept going round and round in her head.

'*That's what we do in Whitby. We look after each other.*'

It really was astonishing how the people of Whitby had rallied against Hermione Nethergate – a spectacular show of solidarity against a common enemy. It made Liz proud to be part of the community. Yet... a murder had taken place in the very heart of that same community, a murder that was no closer to being solved than it had been the night it had happened.

Now that she knew them better, Liz honestly didn't believe that any of the *Stella Mae* crew could have killed Daniel Holliday – even Christian Petit. He might have brawled with Daniel just days before he died, but that was to protect his wife's honour, and his tenderness with his daughter made Liz think he was an unlikely killer. Yet *somebody* had murdered Daniel. The autopsy proved he was dead when he went in the water. Perhaps Bill Williams was right; perhaps Daniel had hit his head fatally on something on deck before falling overboard? Whatever it was that hit him, it had to have been a brutal blow if it killed him instantly. But the forensic search had found nothing on board that could have potentially caused such an injury.

She turned onto her side in another attempt to relax. Even though the night was chilly, she felt hot and uncomfortable, as if her head were full of bees. She stuck one foot out of the bed to try to cool down.

By rights, Daniel Holliday shouldn't have washed up in the harbour at all. Not if the *Stella Mae* was really at Sheringham Shoal at midnight when he'd texted Catriona. Perhaps Skipper had been mistaken about the location? Or perhaps he'd been lying? Liz couldn't imagine him as a murderer. But why else would he lie if he hadn't had anything to do with Daniel's death?

Tilly's voice chimed unexpectedly in her head.

'Loose talk costs lives. We're all in this together.'

We're all in this together.

Holy crap! Liz sat up suddenly, eliciting a groan of protest from Benedict. She lay back down again immediately, her brain whirring in her head. What if... what if Daniel Holliday had never been on the *Stella Mae* at all? What if Skipper and the rest of the crew had only *said* he was? What if Daniel had gone into the water somewhere else entirely? It was an outrageous idea, but perhaps not *so* outrageous in the light of the town's rebellion against Hermione Nethergate. What on earth would prompt Skipper and his crew to tell such an extravagant lie and maintain it even in the face of a police investigation?

They had to be protecting someone. But who?

It was pretty clear that Daniel and Catriona's marriage had been rocky, even if Catriona and Billy weren't having an affair, as now seemed likely. Dora Spackle had mentioned Daniel came to stay with her whenever he and Catriona had a row. His comments about Juliette Petit showed he didn't have a lot of respect for women, and that was further supported by the fact that he had two wives! She thought about poor Amanda Poulson in her nurse's scrubs and bubble gum lipstick. Catriona was still totally in the dark about her and about Daniel's secret other life. Not to mention his daughter! How would she react if she found out?

Liz sat up again.

Bubble gum lipstick!

'What the...' Benedict stirred. 'What's happening?'

'Nothing.' She patted him soothingly on the shoulder. 'Go back to sleep. Everything's fine.'

Everything *was* fine. At last, a picture was beginning to form...

IT TOOK Liz a little while the next morning to get fully into gear. She absent-mindedly opened the oven to get some milk before realising what she was doing. She tutted and went to the fridge.

'Is everything okay?' asked Niall, shovelling egg onto his fork. 'You look a bit discombobulated.'

'I'm fine. I just had a bit of trouble getting to sleep last night.'

'Really?' Benedict gave her a warm look. 'I thought you'd sleep like a baby.'

Liz blushed.

Niall, if he'd heard, pretended he hadn't. He cleared his plate and clapped his hands at the twins, who were finishing their cereal.

'Come on, you two, chop-chop! Get your stuff together, or you'll make me late.'

'You don't need to take us to school,' sulked Lukasz. 'We're not babies.'

'No.' Liz snorted. 'You're Harry Houdini.'

'Who's Harry Houdini?'

Benedict buttered his toast. 'A famous escapologist and magician. He used to get out of chains and escape from locked tanks of water.'

'Sick!' cried Lukasz.

'I want to be an escapologist when I grow up,' decided Eryk.

'I thought you wanted to be a poker player?' said Liz.

'Nah. Too easy. I like the sound of getting out of chains and tanks of water. Can we put sharks in there, too?'

Liz shot Benedict a loaded look – the boys really didn't need any ideas putting in their heads.

Benedict just grinned.

'What are your plans for the day, Liz?' asked Niall.

'Nothing much,' she lied. 'Now that Benbow is finished, I'm at a bit of a loose end.'

'I'm sure you'll find something to do,' said Benedict.

The cottage was very quiet when everyone had gone. Liz washed the breakfast things and put them away, then put on her coat and woollens to take Nelson for a quick walk to the end of Henrietta Street. When they got back, she settled him in his basket with a treat and set off out again.

She headed for New Quay Road. The spring-like feel hadn't lasted long – the temperature had dropped again. Liz's breath curled in the air, and the cobbles were frosty underfoot, but luckily her old salt-stained boots had a decent grip. As she crossed the swing bridge to the west side of town, she was surprised to see that the *Stella Mae* had gone. It was odd not seeing it there after all this time. She supposed Skipper and his crew must have taken her out – they had a living to earn, after all. She hoped Skipper would somehow find a way to keep the *Stella*. She couldn't really imagine him crewing for anyone else. Would he keep his nickname? She had no idea what his real name was.

When she got to New Quay Road, she saw the curtains were closed at the windows to Catriona's flat. Liz rang the doorbell and waited. To her surprise, Catriona answered almost straight away, dressed in sweats, and wearing trainers.

'Mrs Mac, you're lucky you caught me. I was just going for a run.'

'Don't let me stop you. I can come back.'

Catriona peered out the door. 'It looks cold out there.'

'It is a bit. You'll have to watch you don't slip on the frost.'

Catriona grimaced. 'You know what, I might go later. Come in.'

Liz took off her coat and woollens in the hall and followed Catriona into the kitchen. The young woman seemed a lot more cheerful than she'd been the last time Liz had visited. The kitchen was tidier, too – there were no takeaway cartons or empty wine bottles on the counters.

'I gave myself a bit of a talking-to,' said Catriona, catching

Liz's look. 'It's no good just moping about in here, is it? I'm trying to get out and about more.'

'Good idea,' said Liz. 'Not easy, though.'

'Everyone's been very kind. And it's easier now Dad's cleared out all Danny's clothes.'

Liz could definitely sympathise with that. She hadn't been able to bring herself to get rid of Mark's clothes for a full six months after he'd died, and in the end, had only done it because she was selling the house. Psychologically, it was a momentous step.

'Milk and sugar?'

'Just milk, please.'

As Catriona busied herself with the kettle and cups, Liz tried to think of a way to steer the conversation round to the subject she wanted to talk about. She realised, however, there was no way to raise it naturally. She would just have to come out and ask. She was just about to open her mouth to say something when they both heard a noise in the hall – the front door opening and closing. Liz looked at Catriona.

Catriona's eyes had widened and were fixed, like a deer in the headlights, on the kitchen door. She started towards it, but it opened before she got there.

'The door wasn't locked, so I let myself in. You really should be more care...' The woman's words tailed off as first she spotted Catriona's horrified expression... and then Liz. She frowned. 'You,' she said.

'Hello, Amanda.' Liz had the answer she wanted, without even having to ask. It *had* been Amanda's pink lipstick on Catriona's crockery the last time she visited. And, presumably, it had also been Amanda hiding in the bedroom.

Catriona stared at them both, aghast.

Amanda took a step towards them and glared at Catriona. 'Why didn't you text me and tell me she was here?'

'I wasn't expecting you until this afternoon.'

Amanda glared at Liz and put her hands on her hips. 'Well? Are you happy now?'

It dawned on Liz, belatedly, that she was in a dangerous situation. She hadn't told anyone about her plan to visit Catriona, and here she was in the presence of one – maybe even two – murderers.

22

The three women stared at each other like gunslingers, each waiting for someone else to make the first move. It was Amanda who spoke first.

'I suppose you're jumping to conclusions now.'

'Conclusions?' asked Liz.

'About Dan.'

Liz said nothing. It wasn't too much of a leap to imagine the two women deciding to murder their husband when they found out about his bigamy. What had happened after that, exactly, was less clear.

Amanda was watching her face carefully. Too late, Liz realised she probably should have said something.

'Grab her!' Amanda rushed towards Liz. After a start of surprise, Catriona ran to help her.

'Grab her feet. I'll tie her hands with my scarf.'

Liz struggled, but not too much. She didn't want to tip an already dangerous situation into an irredeemable one.

'Put her on the chair.'

Liz was hauled up onto one of the kitchen chairs. She looked at her captors.

'What do we do now?' Catriona asked Amanda.

'How should I know? I've never done anything like this before. We can't just leave her, though. She'll go to the police.'

'Can I make a suggestion?'

The two women stared at her.

'Why don't you just tell me what happened?' Liz knew she probably should scream – someone in the block of flats was bound to hear her – but she didn't want to push the two women into doing something they would regret.

'We should gag her,' said Catriona, in dismay.

'You don't need to. I promise I won't scream.' Liz kept her tone as calm as she could. 'Let's just have a nice cup of tea and talk about this.'

'A nice cup of tea?' repeated Amanda, incredulous. 'How will that help?' She glowered at Liz. 'Give me one good reason why we shouldn't kill you.'

'Kill her?' squeaked Catriona. 'I don't want to kill her!'

Amanda flashed her a look of fury. 'Why not? It's her own fault. Sticking her nose into other people's business.'

Liz really couldn't argue with that. It was – absolutely – all her own fault, and she had – absolutely – stuck her nose into other people's business.

'This is terrible.' Catriona dropped into one of the other kitchen chairs and put her head in her hands. As Amanda looked down at her, uncertainty and regret flickered on her face.

Liz saw her opportunity. 'I might be able to help.'

'How?' Amanda turned on her angrily. 'Are you some kind of irritating fairy godmother? Do you have a magic wand in your pocket?'

Liz shrugged. 'What harm could it do to tell me what really happened? I can't see either of you as cold-blooded killers.'

'We're not.' Catriona lifted her head from her hands. 'We're really not.'

'So it was an accident?'

'Not exactly. But we didn't mean to kill him. He just—'

'Catriona!' Amanda snapped at her. 'Don't say anything incriminating!'

Catriona's voice rose. 'Don't you think it's gone past that already? We have this woman tied to a chair.'

'Yes, but—'

'Face it, Amanda. We're going to prison. We *all* are.'

All? Liz frowned. Had her conspiracy theory been correct?

'And that's exactly why we shouldn't tell her anything,' countered Amanda. 'Don't you see? It's not just about us.'

'So, what are you going to do? Beat her to death? Throttle her with that scarf? Make her drink bleach?'

Liz felt the blood drain from her face.

Catriona continued, 'I'm not going to kill her, and I'm not going to let you kill her, either.'

'But—'

'Oh, for God's sake.' Catriona untied Liz's hands. 'Put the bloody kettle on.'

FIVE MINUTES LATER, they were all sitting around the kitchen table, drinking tea, as if nothing had happened. Liz peered into her mug. She hadn't seen Amanda put anything in it except milk, but... Catriona caught her look.

'Sorry,' she said. 'About the bleach thing.' She shook her head. 'It just popped into my head. I don't know why. We would never do that.'

The look Amanda gave Liz wasn't quite so reassuring. Liz tried not to think too hard about it.

'So,' she began. 'How...?'

Catriona looked at Amanda. 'Do you want to tell her what happened?'

Amanda sighed heavily. 'Like I told you when you came to my house in York, I found out about Catriona when I saw her and Dan together in Whitby. It was a complete fluke that I spotted them. A chance in a million... and when I confronted Dan about it, he admitted everything. He said it was a relief to come clean... and then... nothing.' Amanda clenched and unclenched her hands. 'He made no real apology, or promise to give Cat up, or even a hint that he might try to sort it all out. He just expected me to brush the whole thing under the carpet, like it never happened.'

'But you didn't want to do that?'

'I was tempted to. For Ruby's sake. But in the end, I couldn't. I'm just not made that way.'

Liz could see that. Amanda Poulson was too assertive to let something like that slide. And quite right, too.

Amanda scowled. 'I hated that Dan could think he could just go on making fools of us both.'

'So you told Catriona?'

Amanda nodded. 'It took me a while to pluck up the courage. Almost two weeks. But eventually, I came here and told her everything.'

'I didn't believe her at first. But then she showed me photos. Of her and Danny together. And their little girl...' Catriona broke off and covered her mouth. 'Sorry.'

Amanda reached over the table to squeeze her hand. She gave Catriona a moment to compose herself before she spoke.

'We agreed to confront him together. He'd been out drinking, at the White Horse, so we waited for him to come home.'

'Then we told him he had to leave. Leave both of us.'

'And he didn't take it well?'

'That's putting it mildly.' Catriona's eyebrows rose. 'He was bloody furious.'

'He hit her,' said Amanda.

Catriona saw Liz's look of concern. 'Oh, it wasn't the first time – far from it. Before, though, it had only been his fists. This time, after he'd swung a couple of punches, he picked up a carving knife from the sink. I thought he was going to kill me.'

'So did I.' Amanda's expression was bleak. 'So I hit him. I hit him with the first thing that came to hand. I was only trying to stop him from stabbing Cat, but... I hit him really, really hard.' Her breath caught on a sob. 'He didn't stay down, so I hit him again. We couldn't believe it when we saw he wasn't breathing.' Her face crumpled.

Now it was Catriona's turn to put a comforting hand on Amanda's. 'It's okay. You didn't mean to do it.'

'No, I didn't,' sobbed Amanda. 'But that's still manslaughter, isn't it?'

Catriona turned to Liz. 'You can see that I couldn't let her go to prison? She has Ruby to look after. And Danny... he didn't deserve to die, but it was still his fault. All of it.'

'I can see that.' Liz nodded. 'So what did you do when you realised he was dead?'

'I was completely numb.' Amanda shook her head. 'I had no idea what to do.'

'We talked about calling the police and the ambulance,' continued Catriona, 'but in the end, I called Billy instead. He's my best friend. He didn't like Danny. He knew he sometimes hit me.' She paused and wiped her face with her sleeve. 'Anyway, it was Billy who came up with the plan. We waited until the next night. It was horrible... horrible... having Danny in here all that time... But the next night, Billy and Potsy took him to the harbour, carrying him between them, like he was passed-out drunk. No one suspected anything – it wasn't the first time they'd got him home that way. Then they took him, and the poker Amanda had killed him with, to the three-mile ground in Grunty Gillespie's little fishing coble.'

'They scuppered the coble after,' said Amanda. 'They couldn't risk leaving any forensic evidence.'

'That was the day before the storm?' asked Liz.

'Yes.'

Another piece of the puzzle fell into place. Poor old Grunty thought his boat had been lost in the storm – he mustn't have realised it was missing the day before.

'Billy spoke to Skipper. When he told him what had happened, he agreed to help. Billy took Danny's phone on the *Stella Mae* when they went out the next day, texted me at midnight, then dropped it overboard. Everyone agreed to say that Danny had been on board with them.'

'So... the whole crew was in on it?'

'Everyone except Christian Petit,' said Catriona. 'Nobody knew him that well, and they didn't know if they could trust him to keep the secret. They all pretended that Dan had a stomach bug and was in the toilet. Until the storm hit, then they were all too busy to worry about what everyone else was doing anyway.'

That explained a lot. It explained the whole business about the boat being at Sheringham Shoal, and also why Skipper had dismissed Christian after the fatal trip. If he'd stayed on the crew, no one else would ever have been able to mention what had really happened. There was a serious possibility that someone might slip up and accidentally incriminate them all. Liz couldn't imagine Skipper taking the decision lightly, but he had fired Christian to protect everyone else.

'It was a good plan,' said Liz. 'A very good plan.'

'Until Danny washed up on the beach.' Catriona exchanged a weary look with Amanda.

'Yeah,' said Amanda. 'We couldn't believe it. Billy and Potsy hadn't taken him out far enough. Usually, it would have been fine, but the sea was really rough for days after the storm. He washed up on Tate Hill beach with all the other flotsam.'

'Technically,' interrupted Catriona, 'he was jetsam. Having been thrown overboard.'

'Spoken like a fisherman's wife,' said Liz.

'A fisherman's widow,' corrected Catriona. 'One of them, anyway.'

No one smiled at the joke, not even Catriona. It was too raw to be truly funny.

'Luckily,' said Amanda, 'the police didn't think him washing up on the beach like that was suspicious. Not at first, anyway.'

'But then DI Flint started asking questions about tides and where the *Stella Mae* had actually been when Dan sent his text to me.'

'Someone must have tipped her off about the tides,' added Amanda.

'Ah.' Liz pulled a face. A guilty face.

Amanda spotted it and glared at her. 'I might have known. You really are a world-class nosy parker.'

Catriona flashed her a warning look. 'In the end, the police didn't really follow up on it, anyway. There was no way they could prove where the *Stella Mae* was at midnight, so it didn't make much difference. It just gave us a few sleepless nights.'

Amanda glared again at Liz. 'Thanks for that.'

'Sorry.' She really was sorry. Sorry for them both, for Amanda's little girl, and the whole terrible mess Daniel had created.

'So that's it.' Catriona spread her hands. 'The whole story.'

Liz sighed. Try as she might, she couldn't see how it was going to end happily for anyone. 'I suppose the million-dollar question is, what are you going to do now?'

Catriona gave her a sideways look. 'That's really up to you, isn't it?'

'What?'

'Well... we're not going to go to police and confess.'

'Definitely not,' said Amanda.

'But we're not going to kill you, either.'

'Aren't we?' asked Amanda. Liz couldn't tell if she was joking.

'No.' Catriona's answer left no room for argument.

Amanda grinned at Liz. 'We're not going to kill you. Apparently.'

Catriona continued, looking at Liz, 'So... the *real* million-dollar question is what are *you* going to do now?'

23

Unsurprisingly, Liz didn't sleep much that night. Catriona and Amanda had promised they would face the consequences if she went to the police and told them everything. Liz knew that was what she *should* do, yet... she'd asked for some time to think about it.

The next morning, Benedict was equally hollow-eyed at the breakfast table. All her tossing and turning had kept him awake, too.

'Perhaps you should ask the doctor for something to help you sleep?' he suggested.

'I don't think it's a permanent state of affairs. I just have a lot on my mind at the moment.'

'Oh?' He frowned. 'Want to tell me about it? A problem shared is a problem halved.'

Liz laughed. 'Not in my experience.' As far as she was concerned, a problem shared was usually doubled. Or even multiplied many times. She thought about Catriona and Amanda, who had managed to involve half the town in their particular 'problem'.

Benedict was silent for a moment, looking thoughtfully at her. 'You're not still thinking about Middlesbrough, are you?'

'What?'

'About me and Gillian? It was all perfectly innocent, you know.'

'Oh, I know that.' She dismissed it with a flap of her hand. In the end, she'd decided to give him the benefit of the doubt.

'I'm glad to hear it.' But his words were contradicted by the look on his face. A flicker of irritation? Disappointment? It was gone in an instant, before Liz had the chance to pin it down.

He stood up and put his cereal bowl in the sink. 'It's quiet this morning. Makes a nice change.'

It was Saturday, and the boys were sleeping in. So was Niall, who'd worked a late shift at the Duke of York the night before.

'What do you fancy doing today?' he asked. 'We could take a run out to Scarborough with the boys if you fancy?'

She was about to answer when Benedict's phone rang. He checked the caller ID.

'It's Caroline Burlington,' he said. 'Why's she calling me on a Saturday?'

'You'll never know if you don't answer it.'

He pulled a face at her and accepted the call. 'Hi, Caroline... yes... yes... okay...'

Liz eavesdropped as she cleared her own dirty dishes away, but it was hard to get the gist of the conversation.

'Okay... thanks for letting me know... That's brilliant news.' He hung up and turned to Liz triumphantly. 'They're releasing Gryzna this afternoon!'

'Oh my God! Has she won her appeal?'

Benedict nodded. 'That's it. She's officially a free woman.'

It was the best news Liz had had for months.

She woke the boys and Niall to tell them. When the

cottage had calmed down again – which was quite some time later – she rang everyone else to give them the news, too.

After that, it was 'all hands on deck'.

Iris volunteered to picked up Gryzna's key from Tilly and give her flat a proper clean and air out – that was, after all, her area of expertise. Tilly and Mags closed the café to plan a Welcome Home party, which Mags immediately started baking for. Benedict arranged a time for him to pick up Gryzna in Middlesbrough, then headed to the cash and carry with the long list Tilly and Mags had given him. Niall did his best to keep the boys occupied, and help them pack, while Liz headed to the supermarket to pick up some groceries for Gryzna's fridge.

She was glad to get out in the fresh air and have some time to think.

It was still early, so the old part of town wasn't too busy. Weak sunlight shone down on its cobbled streets, while seagulls wailed overhead and hopped about on the pavements in search of scraps. Liz hadn't gone very far when she realised, with some surprise, that she was too hot. She took off her hat and gloves and pushed them into her pockets. Perhaps spring was on its way after all?

It was a tremendous relief knowing that Gryzna was safe, and that she wouldn't be separated from the boys. Liz had to admit she was also happy to be able to relinquish her own responsibility. She had no idea how Gryzna managed with the boys on her own. She seemed to have more of a laissez-faire attitude than Liz, which was probably necessary for her own sanity.

Someone stepped out of the baker's onto the pavement just as Liz was passing. They did the classic pavement dodge, mirroring each other's movements, before Liz realised it was Dora Spackle, with her shopping trolley.

'For heaven's sake, get out of my way, woman,' snapped Dora.

'And a very good morning to you, too.'

Dora stuck her nose in the air and marched past. Liz had to smile. It was clearly back to business as usual, in spite of everything that had happened with the key and Amanda in York. Liz wondered how Dora would take it if she knew Catriona and Amanda had killed Daniel. Not well, probably. As things stood, Liz thought Dora would probably return all Daniel's documents to Amanda, and might even want to get to know Ruby, who, after all, was her only living relative. But that was unlikely if Amanda went to prison. In that case, Ruby would probably end up in care, like Eryk and Lukasz.

Before going to the supermarket, Liz crossed the bridge and headed into the town centre for flowers. As she passed Howson's fish shop, she saw Billy and Potsy in their usual spot on the windowsill. She realised she'd been so deep in thought as she'd crossed the swing bridge she'd forgotten to check if the *Stella Mae* had returned from her fishing trip.

Potsy beamed at her. 'Morning, Mrs Mac. Lovely day, isn't it?'

'It is. Morning, Billy.'

'Morning.' Billy returned her greeting laconically and watched her as she passed. Liz wondered if Catriona had told him what had happened the day before. Her decision – whatever it was – would affect him and Potsy, too. They had, after all, disposed of Daniel's body. What was it they called it, an accessory after the fact? She could feel the weight of Billy's gaze on her all the way down Baxtergate. It was something of a relief when she turned left to Station Square, to the florist's shop.

After buying Gryzna a lovely bunch of narcissi and crocuses – another sign that spring was just around the corner – Liz walked to the supermarket. She only needed to buy the basics – fresh bread, milk, tea, eggs and butter – but she couldn't resist picking up a few little luxuries for her too. A bottle of wine. Box of chocolates. Bubble bath. As a result, she had two pretty hefty carrier bags by the time she came out.

She heaved them towards home, along New Quay Road, being careful to keep her eyes averted from Catriona's flat as she passed. She didn't want to bump into Catriona if she could help it, not when she still hadn't made up her mind what she was going to do.

She was just about to start back over the bridge when she heard someone call her name.

'Liz!'

She looked around. It was Skipper, waving at her from St Ann's Staith. She stopped to let him catch up with her.

'I saw you,' he said, breathless, 'and thought I'd share my good news.'

'Oh?'

'Hermione Nethergate's given me back my shares in the *Stella Mae*.'

'Really?'

'I think the pressure in the town just got too much for her. She was probably fed up of having to go to Sandsend for bread.'

'And of clearing fish heads off her driveway.'

He grinned. 'That too.' He spotted her carrier bags. 'Those look heavy. Let me carry them for you.'

'No, honestly, I'm fine.'

'Are you sure?'

'Very sure, thank you.' She hesitated. 'I'm really pleased about the boat.'

'Thanks. I feel like I can start looking ahead to the future now.'

Liz frowned. That future wasn't going to look too rosy if

she decided to tell the police everything she knew. Skipper had also been an accessory after the fact.

'Thanks for letting me know,' she said. 'I'm really happy for you.'

Skipper hesitated. He seemed reluctant to leave her. He scratched his beard.

'I was wondering... um... if you'd maybe like to come for a drink sometime? Or a meal? I know a nice seafood restaurant out Filey way.'

Liz opened her mouth, but no sound came out. She couldn't have been more surprised if he'd gone down on one knee and asked her to marry him.

Skipper saw her look of consternation. His expression shuttered. 'No worries, if not. I just thought I'd ask. As my old gran used to say "shy bairns get nowt".'

'The thing is... I'm actually involved with someone just now.'

'Ah. I didn't know.' He pulled a regretful face. 'And there was me thinking everyone in this town knew everyone else's business.'

'We haven't been going out long.'

'I see.' His cheeks reddened. 'Oh well, never mind.'

They parted company awkwardly, Skipper heading back to the quayside, and Liz over the bridge.

Liz walked in a daze to Gryzna's flat, which was on Green Lane, at the far end of Church Street. Skipper's interest in her had come completely out of the blue. Had she been giving off 'come hither' signals without realising? She didn't think so. Although... when she really thought about it, she did find him attractive. Attractive in a sea-blown, salty kind of way. Not that she would ever... of course not. She had Benedict. Benedict was much more her type.

Iris was waiting for Liz in the flat, dressed in her cleaner's overalls and wearing Marigold gloves. She pounced on her as soon as she came in the door.

'DO YOU HAVE TEABAGS? I'M GAGGING FOR A BREW.'

'Yes, there's tea and milk. Don't eat any of the biscuits, though. They're for Gryzna.'

Iris peered into one of the bags. 'THEY'RE BOURBONS ANYWAY. I HATE BOURBONS.' She saw that Liz wasn't taking her coat off.

'AREN'T YOU STOPPING?'

Liz frowned. She realised she wasn't. 'No, I'm just going to put these flowers in water; then there's something I need to do.'

24

'Do you think we've overdone it?' Tilly asked Liz, looking doubtfully at the café tables, which were groaning with food. She and Mags had been busy all day, baking pies, cakes and vol au vents, and making sandwiches and pizza. They'd also decorated the café, festooning it with brightly coloured streamers and helium balloons. Kevin was just putting the finishing touches to a big banner that hung from the ceiling that said WELCOME HOME, GRYZNA!

'Not at all,' said Liz. 'I think it's lovely.'

She had to raise her voice to be heard over the noise in the café, where all Gryzna's friends had gathered to welcome her home. Even Caroline Burlington was there, having been persuaded by Benedict that she wouldn't be overstepping her professional boundaries. Liz imagined she was probably already regretting it, as she'd been pinned into a corner by Iris, who was bombarding her with personal questions, while Dickie kept asking her to repeat the answers.

After fixing the banner, Kevin moved on to opening champagne, while Niall was occupied full time keeping the boys off the food, and stopping them from running out into the street every two minutes to see if Benedict and Gryzna were coming. Nelson was tearing around in the middle of it all with his rubber pig, squeaking it at anyone who took any notice of him. It was chaos.

Liz was a little worried that it might be overwhelming for someone who'd been stuck in a detention centre for weeks, but squashed down her misgivings – it was too late to worry about that now.

Tilly gave Liz a sideways look. 'Amanda called me about twenty minutes ago.'

'Did she?'

'She asked me to pass on a message... Thanks.'

'Oh.'

'Thanks for what?'

'For not telling everyone about her and Ruby, I should think.'

'If you say so.' Tilly's eyes narrowed. 'Why do I have a feeling there's something you're not telling—'

'They're here!' squealed Eryk, who was looking out the window.

'Mum!' Lukasz joined him in his dash to the door just as Gryzna and Benedict came in.

'My boys!' Gryzna dropped to her knees to hug them both. She hid her face in their shoulders.

Liz blinked back tears as she watched them, and she wasn't the only one. Tilly, Mags, Dickie, Iris and Niall were all leaking tears, and even Kevin and Benedict looked suspiciously red-eyed. The only completely dry eye in the café belonged to Caroline, who, Liz supposed, was somewhat hardened to such scenes.

Finally, Gryzna got to her feet, the boys still clinging to her. She looked much the same as she always had, a little bit thinner, perhaps, but otherwise unscathed by her ordeal.

'Thank you, everyone!'

Everyone cheered, then pressed round to hug and kiss her. Liz held back, knowing there would be plenty of time to catch up with her later.

Benedict obviously had the same idea. He joined Liz and put his arm around her waist.

'Happy?' he asked.

'Very.'

That wasn't strictly true. She was delighted for Gryzna, of course, and for the boys, but she was finding it hard to shake off an undercurrent of melancholy. After dropping Gryzna's shopping at the flat, Liz had gone to see Catriona. She'd told her that, after giving it a lot of thought, she'd decided not to go to the police. Daniel was now beyond anyone's help, and everyone else would lose if she told the police how he had died – two families would be blown apart, a little girl would go into care, and half the town would be implicated in the fallout. Liz wouldn't be able to live with herself knowing she was the cause of such misery. Catriona had cried with relief and thanked her.

Liz still felt conflicted, but guessed she felt a lot better than she would have done if she'd gone to the police and implicated Catriona, Amanda, Potsy, Billy and Skipper in Daniel's death.

'Penny for them?' Kevin had joined her. Liz realised that Benedict had moved on while she'd been deep in thought, and was now laughing on the other side of the café with Caroline Burlington.

'I'm just thinking how lovely it is to have us all together again.'

'It is.'

There was a long, companionable silence between them as they watched everyone else.

'Aren't you going to ask me about the Daniel Holliday case?' he said eventually.

'Why would I?'

'I thought you were interested? After the tip you gave us about the tides.'

'Not particularly.'

'So you're not at all interested to hear we haven't been able to find a single shred of evidence that points to murder?'

'No.'

'No?' Kevin looked about theatrically. 'Who are you, and what have you done with Liz McLuckie?'

Liz laughed. 'Seriously, I think Daniel probably slipped on deck, hit his head and was washed overboard. Sometimes the simplest answers are the right ones, aren't they?'

'The coroner agrees with you. He's signing it off as misadventure. Flint won't be happy. She's convinced there was dirty work involved.'

'And what do you think?'

He gave her a penetrating look. 'I think a lot of people know more than they're letting on. But what I think isn't really important, is it?'

Liz hesitated. She could ask what made him think that, but decided it might be wiser to change the subject. She saw Eryk approaching with two champagne glasses.

'Are they for us?' she asked.

Eryk nodded. 'Niall told me to bring them to you. I haven't spilled them at all. Well, only a little bit.'

'Thank you.' She took one of the glasses. 'Actually, I need to ask you an important question.' She leaned down to whisper in his ear, 'I don't really smell like cheese, do I?'

Eryk spluttered. 'No! I was just mad at you. You don't smell like cheese at all!'

'That's okay, then. I've been a bit worried about that.'

Eryk was clearly delighted by the thought. Liz hugged him, slopping yet more champagne from her glass.

'A toast!' Niall tapped a knife on his own glass to get everyone's attention. 'Our woman of the hour wants to make a toast!'

Everyone quieted down.

Gryzna looked at them all in turn, her face shining with emotion.

'Thank you, everyone. For fighting so hard for me. I could never have known, when I first came to this country, that I would find such friends here. That I would find a home. A home for me and my boys. So... let us raise a glass and make the most important toast of all...'

Everyone lifted their champagne glasses.

'To friendship,' said Gryzna.

'FRIENDSHIP!'

Liz emptied what was left in her glass in a single gulp.

That was a toast worth making!

AUTHOR'S NOTE

Whitby is a real place – a gorgeous jewel of a town nestled on the North Yorkshire coast, on the edge of the North York Moors National Park. It's most famous for being the birthplace of colonial explorer Captain Cook, and the inspiration for Bram Stoker's gothic masterpiece *Dracula*. For those of you lucky enough to be familiar with the town, I've done my best to keep its geography – its street names and layout – as close to the real thing as possible. I may, however, have made a few mistakes and taken a couple of liberties, for which I hope you'll forgive me.

The White Horse and Griffin Hotel, where Christian Petit gave Daniel Holliday his black eye, and the Duke of York pub where Niall has his bar job are both real pubs, rightly popular with locals and tourists. Similarly, the Magpie Café is famous for its food and excellent service. The Captain Cook Memorial Museum in Grape Lane is worth a visit for anyone with the vaguest curiosity about Whitby's seafaring past. Pannet Park Art Gallery and Museum does indeed house the Whitby council offices, but has no petting zoo. (I feel I should make it completely clear, at this point, that I do not condone the abduction of animals from any zoo of any kind!)

The abbey and St Mary's Church on the East Cliff attract visitors from all over the world. I have tried to describe them as accurately as possible.

You can find the Cholmley allotments by turning right at the top of the 199 steps as Liz did, and following the Donkey Path along the East Cliff. The Cholmley family have been influential in Whitby since the 1500s. They built the mansion house beside the abbey, which is now home to the Abbey House Visitor Centre and Museum, where Dora Spackle is head curator. If you've read my first book in the Kipper series – *Death at the Abbey* – you'll be familiar with the museum and some of its exhibits.

Whitby's donkeys were always a massive attraction on its beaches when I was a little girl. I have a photo of myself, about four years old, sitting proudly on the back of one while my dad held me in place. It's sad to have to report, though, that the donkeys weren't always well looked after. After a hard day standing in all weathers and slogging over sand with not-always-well-behaved children on their backs, they were taken up to their field on the East Cliff, up the extremely steep cobbled track that runs parallel to the abbey steps. They must have been permanently exhausted. Although some of the donkeys' owners might have treated their animals humanely, that wasn't always the case. It's probably for the best that beach donkeys are now a thing of the past.

Kipper Cottage and Gull Cottage are based on the two cottages closest to Fortune's Smokehouse, on Henrietta Street. Iris's Benbow Cottage is in Neptune Yard, based on

Kiln Yard, which can be found at the bottom of the abbey steps. The Anchorage Retirement Home and the Full Moon Café are my own inventions, although Sandgate, where the café is located, is always worth a visit. It's packed with fascinating little shops, including the Whitby Glass workshop, where they make the town's famous Lucky Ducks.

The RNLI Lifeboat Station on the Fish Pier is in active service and has a live webcam. At any given moment you can take a real-life peek out into Whitby harbour, to check out the weather and general comings and goings of boats on the water.

I hope you've enjoyed spending time in Whitby with Liz McLuckie, and that you'll join her for her next adventure in the Kipper Cottage Mystery series – *Death on the West Cliff*.

Until then, happy armchair sleuthing!

———

If you'd care to leave a review on Amazon they are enormously helpful in getting books discovered by new readers and I would be grateful for you thoughts.

ABOUT THE AUTHOR

Jan lives just outside Edinburgh with her husband, three kids, a one-eye whippet and a fat black pug. Born in a colliery village in the North East of England, she cut her literary teeth on the great storytellers of the 60's and 70's - Wilbur Smith, Frank Yerby, Mary Renault, and Sergeanne Golon. She began her writing career as an advertising copywriter, and has since had novels published by Random House and HarperCollins, and original audio series produced by Audible UK. She also writes for tv.

Jan enjoys psychological thrillers and crime fiction of all kinds, from the coziest of cozies to the blackest of noirs.

You can find Jan at www.kippercottagemysteries.co.uk

ALSO BY JAN DURHAM

Kipper Cottage Mysteries

Death at the Abbey (Book 1)

Death at Neptune Yard (Book 2)

Death at the Feast (Book 3)

Death at the Anchorage (Book 4)

Death on the Stella Mae (Book 5)

Printed in Great Britain
by Amazon

19435917R00123